STATIONS OF THE CROSS

Paintings by Chris Gollon
Stories by Sara Maitland

continuum

Continuum
The Tower Building
11 York Road
London SE1 7NX

Suite 704
80 Maiden Lane
New York
NY 10038

www.continuumbooks.com

First published 2009

British Library Cataloguing-in-Publication Data
A catalogue record for this book is available from the British Library.
ISBN 978 0 8264 0568 5
Designed and typeset by Benn Linfield
Printed and bound by Ashford Press, Hampshire

Contents

For David Tregunna,
with thanks

Introduction

When I have to go to London, I usually stay in the Rectory at St John on Bethnal Green. It is a place I like to be. It has numerous practical advantages — including free parking and a very handy tube station — but actually they are not the point. Alan Green and Sabine Butzlaff are very old friends and they have a gift of hospitality, which makes staying with them easy. There is always excellent food, lots of drink and a warm welcome. It is also a place where people are talking about and doing things I find interesting. One of those things has been about the meeting-points, the competition and the exchanges between religion and art. It is stimulating, exciting and loving. Because I have stayed there over many years, I have also come to know the congregation and the huge, worn church.

This is how I encountered Chris Gollon's Stations of the Cross quite early in the process that Fr Green describes in his Afterword to this book. I very quickly came to share the vision and enthusiasm that has made them possible. I was moved, both by these extraordinary paintings and by the courage of the parish in commissioning them. I will be honest now and admit that I did not think they could pull it off. So much did I doubt it that I committed myself very early on to paying for the eighth Station if they got the first seven Stations sponsored and completed. I picked that Station because it was safely far down the line, but also because my first novel was called *Daughter of Jerusalem* so it felt appropriate. I have seldom been so pleased to be wrong.

For a long time I have been interested in the Stations of the Cross as a resource for prayer, but also as a way in to an older theology of the Incarnation that I find increasingly interesting and balancing; something that is both communal and private, active and contemplative, and profoundly inclusive. As Gollon's paintings emerged one by one, I discovered that engaging with them deepened my own prayer and gave me a stronger sense of the humanity (the physical human-being-ness) of Jesus.

The Stations of the Cross are a traditional Christian devotion. Most Roman Catholic churches and many Anglican ones have a series of Stations round the walls of the church, or outside along a prearranged walk. Monasteries and convents, for example, often have their Stations placed around their cloisters. The representation of each Station ranges from simple in the extreme — a small, plain, wooden cross with a number on or beside it — through to elaborate, colourful, baroque statuary. But, regardless of place or style, their intention has always been to allow people to meditate on the passion of Jesus, in order to bring home to each Christian their own great value in the eyes of a God who would undergo this painful, humiliating and drawn-out process out of love for them. At different times the faithful have been exhorted to different emotional responses to this act — gratitude, compassion, penitence, reparation, sorrow — but, at the centre of it, we are invited to look at one of the stories about a God who loves us. For people who find it all too gruesome, it is worth remembering that the Stations grew out of the same spiritual movement as the Crib Scene, which offers another "take" on the divine generosity. Both the Nativity Tableau and the Stations of the Cross were made popular by the Franciscans, who wanted to bring a deeply human Jesus into the consciousness of illiterate and impoverished communities. (It is also worth bearing in mind that, at the time, the pain and danger of childbirth were so much greater than now that it is very unlikely that many people would have seen the Bethlehem crib scene as "sweet" in quite the way that we do.) Babies are still born into frightening poverty, there is still homelessness and the ruthless removal of people by governments and the attendant risks to babies and mothers — Jesus experienced that. There is still torture, and scourging, and imperialist invasions supported by local interests; there are still unjust judges, cruel punishments, and wretched deaths — Jesus experienced that. It is not that Christians of earlier generations were insensitive; Teresa of Avila admits that "our temperament or some indisposition will not always allow us to think of the Passion, because of its painfulness . . . Certainly it is not always that one can bear to think of such great trials as those which he suffered." It seems to have been, rather, a clear-sighted recognition of the reality of political oppression, physical pain and mental anguish, and Jesus' sharing in that.

The form in which we now have the Stations took a while to settle down — even the number has varied (the maximum that I can find is sixty-four). From the seventeenth century until very recently, the Stations became standardised in the shape and order in which Chris Gollon has painted them here. However, the Second Vatican Council (1962–1965) emphasised the centrality of the Bible in Catholic teaching, and endeavoured valiantly to purge Catholic practice of non-biblical and mythological material. This created a problem for the traditional Stations of the Cross because, of the existing fourteen Stations, five (numbers 3, 4, 6, 7 and 9) have no scriptural basis whatsoever and number 13 is felt to have been so over-elaborated as to have lost touch with its Biblical source. In consequence, a different series of "scriptural" Stations was proposed and was authorised for use by the present Pope in 2007.

The new sequence is:

Jesus in the Garden of Gethsemane
Jesus is betrayed by Judas and arrested
Jesus is condemned by the Sanhedrin
Jesus is denied by Peter
Jesus is judged by Pilate
Jesus is scourged and crowned with thorns
Jesus takes up his cross
Jesus is helped by Simon to carry his cross
Jesus meets the women of Jerusalem
Jesus is crucified

Jesus promises his kingdom to the good thief
Jesus entrusts Mary and John to each other
Jesus dies on the cross
Jesus is laid in the tomb.

Perhaps surprisingly, St John's Parish and Gollon did not follow this schema, but stuck with the dark and painful traditional pattern, including those Stations that are without Biblical authority.

It has in addition become increasingly common to add to the end of the sequence a fifteenth Station, representing Resurrection — the risen Jesus and the joy of Easter. Gollon's new Stations for St John's do not include a Station for the resurrection; instead, as Fr Green describes, the Stations end with the dead Jesus in his grave and the church doors leading out into the East End of London.

For me these were important and courageous decisions, rather than pious and conservative ones.

There is an immediate, practical problem with the new, scriptural Stations: they cannot be "performed", or made as a pilgrimage in real time in the way in which the old ones can. The fourteen traditional Stations can be mapped on the ground and walked in a single "movement" as Jesus walked them; there is no inconvenient "overnight" hiatus to address. They flow into and through each other in natural rhythm, which starting the sequence the evening before in Gethsemane cannot do. Fr Green has written about the centrality of pilgrimage in the parish's vision for their Stations, and the traditional Stations offer this in a way that the new ones do not.

This problem becomes even clearer if the Resurrection is pulled in to the narrative. Jesus' own community of friends had to endure three whole days of waiting, of sadness, of loss and of anxiety. They thought he was dead; we need to enter into that with them, if we want to experience fullness of joy at all. The immediate, unbroken move to a Station of the Resurrection calls into question the reality of Jesus' death. It gives, in an odd sense, credibility to the accusation that Christianity offers only an escape out of the pain of the world, rather than a profound engagement with it. Resurrection should not be easy consolation in the Church, but a longed-for renewal in the world.

There is another reason why I am deeply contented with the choice that St John's made. I have a joyful and abiding confidence in the mediaeval narrative sensibility. There is a deep and delightful rightness about the stories they told.

John's Gospel gives us permission to add things on with the explicit observation that not everything Jesus did is included in the Gospel because, "were every one of them to be written down, I suppose that the world itself could not contain the books that would be written" (John 21:25). Interestingly, many modern theologians urge us to "read between the lines" (Elizabeth Fiorenza's phrase) when trying to tackle contemporary ethical issues. The mediaeval Church was remarkably skilled in this when tackling psychological issues, as we see in many of the lives of the saints.

It is plausible, indeed likely, that a tired man who needs help carrying his cross (Biblical) might fall over on closely-packed, uphill streets. But there is more to it than that: the psalms frequently use the image of stumbling and falling as something from which God will protect his favoured ones. Satan used Ps 91:11–12 to tempt Jesus in the wilderness, with the promise that God "will give his angels charge over you . . . on their hands they will bear you up lest you strike your foot against a stone." How better to demonstrate Jesus' abandonment and desolation than these repeated falls? And at the same time there is a prophetic element: Ps 35 says, "At my stumbling they gathered in glee." How better to hint to the individual that Jesus is mocked and despised and laughed at than by these repeated falls? Three falls — for the three temptations, for the "world, the flesh and the devil." The Stations of the Cross were created by a society that had an impressively deep range of Biblical reference, and also understood at a profound level that art (paintings, stories, music, architecture) could in many circumstances reflect this better than abstract thought or rational explanation ever could.

Indeed, in my telling of the stories of the Stations, I take up a number of ancient associations. In particular, the identification of Veronica (the woman who wiped Jesus' face with a cloth in Station 6) with the woman with the haemorrhage whom Jesus cures when she touches the hem of his garment is no invention of mine; it was well established in the mediaeval Church. It makes such good narrative sense, and pulls us so directly into the world in which Jesus lived as well as died, that I have embraced it with delight.

So I believe the traditional fourteen Stations offer particular riches that modernity stands in need of, and I have so much enjoyed the way Gollon has interpreted the old stories, both as an exercise in the contemporary and as a challenge to our current sensibility — which wants to be protected from too much darkness by "quick fix" solutions, and which has lost the ability to create deep images and stories.

But there was another aspect to all this. I felt myself profoundly challenged as a writer by Gollon's ability to hold together a long tradition and simultaneously to represent it in a completely contemporary way. Since the late 1980s I have been trying, in various ways, to write stories that are both genuinely works of literature and equally genuinely works of theology — a theology of the imagination; an "artful theology", as the feminist theologian Angela West has described it. In 1989, BBC Radio 4 commissioned me to write a sequence of stories for Holy Week, and I wrote five stories about the women who encountered Jesus in one way or another during the last week of his life. I tried both to stay faithful to the biblical narrative and at the same time to bring a contemporary life and sensibility to the individual women involved. These were real women, not pious silhouettes, and they deserved real voices, real stories.

Encountering Gollon's Stations, I knew that he had gone further than I had. Stylistically and emotionally, Gollon has created a Jesus who is human. I have come to think that there are real advantages, when working on themes about the Incarnation, in having an artist who is not an active Christian or, try as we will, the "God-bits" creep back in. (Hence, I suspect, the innumerable images of a rather soppy-looking Jesus, tidily and gracefully — if non-anatomically — pinned to his cross, with not a wrinkle of pain on his forehead.) It is almost impossible to inflict pain on God. Gollon does not have these inhibitions — and it shows in the powerful images. I think it would be nearly impossible for a Christian artist to use his own son as his model for Jesus, and yet, by doing so, Gollon is able to bring some of the complex emotions of parenthood to the work. I wanted to get inside this power as a writer as well as a Christian.

So these stories have become for me a process of engaging with Gollon's images — my stories are all responses to his pictures, as well as to the primary narratives his pictures illustrate.

There is one exception to this. Gollon paints the actual crucifixion differently from how I write it. He has four nails, two going through the palms of Jesus' hands, and one through each foot, with the legs stretched downwards. I write about the nails going through the base of the hands, the knees flexed upwards and a single nail pinning both feet. I had planned to follow Gollon's lead, but in the end I could not write it that way. It would not be physically possible, as I understand the anatomy, to crucify someone like that. For example, that part of the human hand cannot support the weight of the rest of the body for long enough. There are arguments on both sides – for the tradition and for a more rigorous physical realism. I am not criticising Gollon's choice here, but I found I made a different one. This may in part have something to do with a difference between written and visual forms. Violence and pain are less shocking in written form than in visual forms. To add the different shock of an unfamiliar crucifixion to the already intensely painful content of these images might make praying with them unbearable.

Other than this I have tried to stay as close to the images as I could. This has been fascinating for me, because Gollon's Jesus is not the Jesus of my own imagination even at the simple, visual level. Equally importantly, though, some of the supporting cast are very different from how I have imagined them — both in their physical appearance and in their emotional responses. The clearest example of this is Mary. Of all the stories, I found the one for Station 4 the hardest to write, because of the discrepancy between "my" Mary and Gollon's Mary. I find looking at her turning away while her son looks at her with that deeply ambivalent expression very hard to fathom, and very hard to talk about. I find it hard to give up my own preferred rapt-but-supportive gaze for this strange, fierce exchange. I have tried to persuade myself that this is because I am a mother and Gollon is not — and that therefore, mysteriously, I know better. But this does not work. I do not know how she looked; she is not "mine". What I have learned is that opening myself to his images has actually deepened my own. Not damaged or weakened them, but exactly the opposite: these characters are more real to me now than they were before, because I have had to recognise that I cannot own them.

It was this recognition that led me to add at the end of each story a comment on it by someone else. Most, though not all, of these quotes come from members of the congregation of St John's. They are comments on the images, not the stories, because the speakers had not had an opportunity to read the stories. I hope what they will do is set free all our imaginations so that we can engage with this rich and complex tradition.

Teresa of Avila, *The Life of the Holy Mother Teresa of Jesus,* Chapter XXII (trans. E.Allison Peers; Sheed and Ward 1946).

These stories, with some other attempts at narrative theology, were published in 1995 as a collection of short stories called *Angel and Me* (Continuum).

THE STATIONS

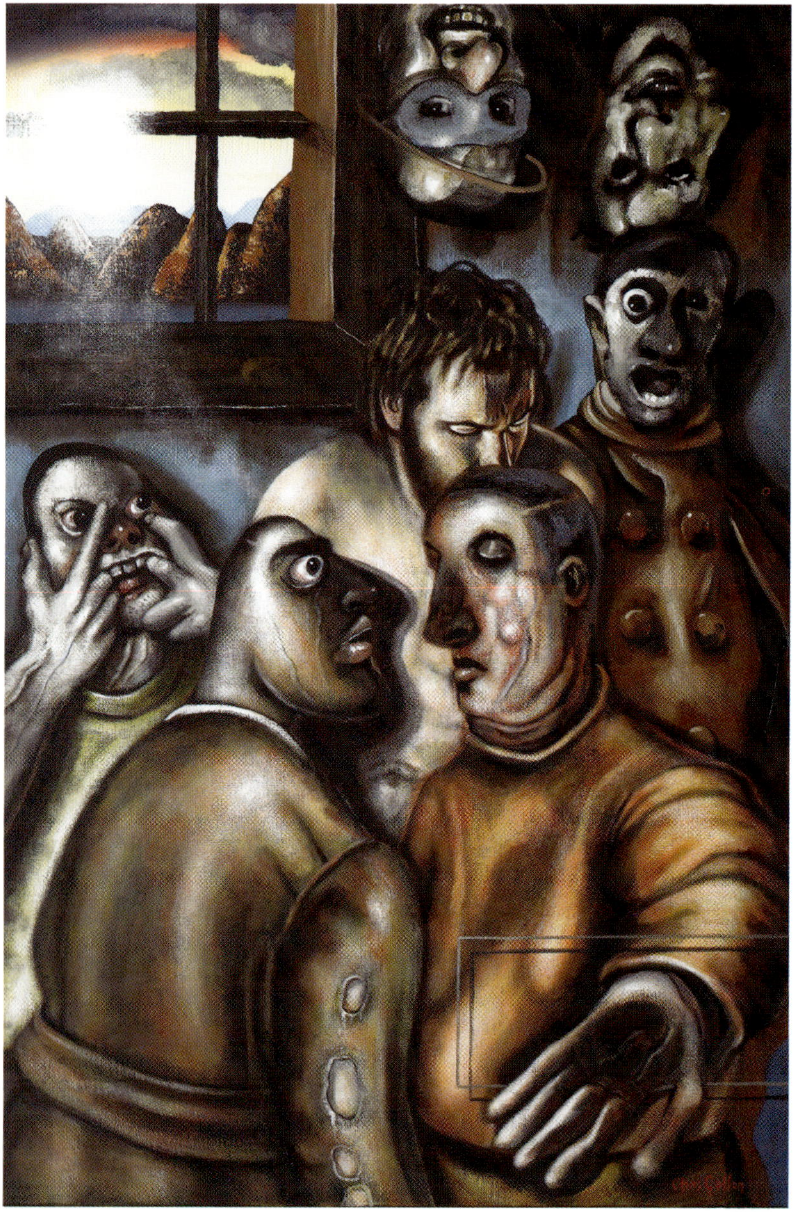

Station 1:
Jesus is condemned to death

It was grotesque.

We were grotesque. I was grotesque. He stayed human. We broke ourselves and we could not break him.

It makes me restless and uneasy.

It was unbearable in the barracks. The mess room was uncomfortable, nervous. The lads were sullen or insolent, and when I left they were beginning to be drunken as well. There'll be fights later. I had to get out of there. I derelicted my duties, like everyone else has done all day today, and went out into the city.

I pretended to myself I was looking for a letter-man, that I would send a letter to my family in Macedonia; and yet I knew it was a solemn holiday for them and there would be no one on the dark streets. It is chilly out here and very dark. There is a mean little wind that catches you at the corners. But it is better than the uneasy bitterness of the barracks. Jerusalem is a very ancient city, but it feels turned in on itself somehow. Perhaps it is because they have no statues – no statues, no painting, no fountains. Tonight the whole city feels restless and uneasy, even though the streets are empty. All day it was noisy, edgy and tense; now it is silent, edgy and tense, and I am not sure which I like least. They disappear into their houses, into the shadows and we are, rather literally, left out in the cold.

I know this city is heaving with people; there is some local festival going on, and once a year they pour in from every corner of the Empire, until there is hardly room to walk in the tight, narrow streets. And the Governor gets nervous because of the crowds, so we are called up from Philippi to show a little Roman muscle, to push the crowds around and to strut Rome's authority in the streets and marketplaces; and they hate us and pretend to ignore us, and we do not make anything easier for anyone, and they hate us. They hate us especially at this feast, which is about their ancient freedom. Their feasts are solemn: dark, somehow, and private, and inside; they are not like ours, which are drunken, and joyful, and outside in the fresh air. They all go into their own houses and the streets are empty and silent. We nearly had a riot this morning, and now the streets are empty. They wanted the killing done but they hate us for doing it. I am restless and uneasy.

It was a travesty. That's not my sort of word, but . . . we are here, they tell us, for Law and Order – the great Roman gifts of civic order, peace, good governance, justice. Not for a trial like that. Top down, I want to think – and it is true, or nearly true. Injustice at the top breeds cruelty at the bottom. The Governor sat there, he sat there with his toga on; with all the stuff, all the Roman stuff – polish and power, shiny Roman stuff. He's elegant, in that posh, urbane, Roman way, with white, soft hands and sophisticated wit; and everyone knew he was shitting himself with terror. He was shameless, and we were ashamed.

He didn't just know that the man was innocent; he said that he was innocent. He spoke with quiet smoothness in that haughty, Roman way, and then had his words translated into a blaring shout – he did not even speak them himself to the crowd.

"I find no fault in him."

Fair enough – though, if our job is to keep the peace, then you could say he was guilty, because there was not a lot of peace in Jerusalem this week, and no question but that he was the centre of it, whatever "it" was – but what do I know? What does the Governor know, come to that?

"I find no fault in him," he said. And, if you know those Roman grandees, you could see that he wanted to be brave – sort of. But he's a stinking, miserable coward. He washed his lily-white hands in a beautiful bronze bowl. He sent for water, warm water so he would not chill his little, pinky fingers, and dried them all elegantly on a bleached linen towel, and said in that lah-de-dah, patrician voice, "I am innocent of this righteous man's blood."

He sounded like a little kid, caught at something naughty, who says, "I didn't do it, it wasn't my fault, and anyway they made me." We were ashamed. It wasn't right. It wasn't Roman law. It was not justice.

Injustice at the top leads to shame at the bottom and shame leads to cruelty. It has left me restless and uneasy.

I never thought about it before today, but now I find myself wondering about the scourging. It's our job – the garrison does the scourging. Everyone who is found guilty of anything (unless, of course, they are a citizen or some grandee) gets scourged. Routine. But today I see the scourging gives us power – gives the front-line troops, who never do anything except obey orders, a bit of power. We choose just how hard the prisoner gets scourged. Within limits, of course; better not kill them, and better not send them out looking all clean and fresh and hunky-dory. But still, we get to comment on what we think of the judgement. I think that is why some of us like it, like doing the scourging. You see really gentle guys – the sort that takes their puppy into the tent at night when it's cold; the sort who are a bit squeamish about wringing a chicken's neck or pushing an old woman out of the way on the street – and they like the scourging. They enjoy it. I've done it – Duty, you say sternly to yourself the first time; and then you tie their arms up to the hook on the pillar and find you are tying them just a little tighter than you need to, just a little higher, because it makes the skin on their backs stretch a bit. You see them flinch before you actually touch them. They are at your mercy. You even have the power to be kind if you want. You can do what you like.

There's another thing. Scourging is the law of course, but when you whip someone like that you break them; you break them down and then you can despise them and that makes whatever you have to do next a lot easier. It's odd, no one likes crucifixions, but most of the lads like scourging – or at least they don't dislike it and some of them really get off on it.

But him, today; they couldn't break him.

I put two of them on the job, just chosen casually. I didn't want to be too gentle because the Governor had made me angry, but they were not like thugs – I thought they would be businesslike and quick, because we wanted to get out there and get the three of them up as early as possible, because of this festival and all the unrest and because, if you are going to do it, you might as well get on with it. But they couldn't break him.

It's like this: when you scourge someone, something inside them falls apart. It's the pain of course, but not just the pain. They are tied to the pillar, with their face against it, so they can't see what's coming. You strut about a bit, flex your whip, lay on hard or less hard – and they can't tell which or when. That unnerves them. Some of them whimper and beg, some of them rage and curse; some close down, cut themselves off, like they've taken some drug or something. There's different ways, but it is all the same – you have got to them, you have broken them, they are made smaller, you feel bigger. But . . . I left the lads to it; went to check the crucifixion detachment were all set, everything in place, all the equipment. Given the situation out there, the mood those people are in, I wasn't risking anything going wrong. So when I came back I could see the two of them were in a funny mood – red-faced, and savage. I watched a moment or two before I understood. They just hadn't got to him. I don't mean he shut down or cut off or whatever it is; and I don't mean it didn't hurt him. You could see it hurt him, but that was all it did – it didn't make him angry, or grovelling, or ashamed, or anything. They'd done a proper job but they couldn't break him. They hadn't made him smaller; they'd made themselves smaller.

So. Yes. OK. It was me. I try to tell myself it was for the two of them – no condemned bloody prisoner was going to make my lads look small. But now, tonight, I know he made me look smaller too, and I wasn't having it. I slapped him about a bit; banged his head against the pillar; prodded the long welts the whips had made. I think the lads were surprised, but not sorry. It didn't do me any good. I untied his hands, spun him round and spat in his face.

"Call yourself a king, then?" I asked him – and the two of them laughed which sort of made me feel better, but he just smiled and said, "No, I didn't. Your Governor did."

The thing was, he just answered the question; not cheeky, not uppity, but certainly not scared, not rattled. He answered the question as though I had asked it to him without any of the nasty sarcastic edge I knew that I had used.

I lost it. I called in the whole battalion. I wound them up good and proper and let them set about him. No violence – not real violence, just mockery and baiting and bullying and swagger. They did not need a lot to get them going, just needed me not to stop them. It was cruel.

They stripped him naked. I don't know why, but these people really hate being naked. They hate it so much they never go to the baths, so they're filthy. Perhaps it's because they do this weird thing to their pricks – sort of nick the end off somehow. We got to see that and to laugh at it. Touch it, discuss it, ask him about it and about Jewish women and didn't they prefer decent Roman men. Then someone produced an old bit of purple stuff, dirty and thrown aside by some officer I expect. They slung it round his shoulders, gave him a stick to hold like a sceptre. Someone twisted up a rough circlet of thorns and crammed it onto his head – when the thorns dug in I saw the tears well up in his eyes, but they were physical tears. Everyone got to hit him and kick him and spit at him – but more it was the verbal abuse.

"Your Majesty...

"Your Royal Highness . . .

"Command and I obey, O King . . ."

That sort of stuff.

We're supposed to respect their religious ideas, which they take ridiculously seriously. "No jokes about religion while in uniform." Top-level orders. So I should have come down sharp and hard on whoever started the worshipping business. One of the charges, trumped up or otherwise, was about him claiming to be a Son of God – a bit like the Emperor, though we won't mention that. It means something pretty serious for the locals, and by rights I should have stopped it. But I let it go and all the lads are down on their knees, laughing and jeering and play-acting worship, praying to him you know, and it was getting a bit filthy – virgin goddesses and that sort of thing; and I look at him, and he's looking at me, and then he smiles.

I've only ever known anyone smile that smile once, and that was my mother, when we boys were doing something naughty – not bad, not wicked, but silly. My mother was a slave; my father manumitted her when she was expecting my oldest brother, so he could marry her and us lot all be born as freemen. She was lovely, my mother, but she could not ever bring herself to be strict with us – she did not have a habit of giving orders, of getting what she wanted, and she loved us to be free enough to be naughty sometimes. She would just smile because we were free. And that was his smile.

And I looked at us and I saw how grotesque we were. We were scum. Because something in him was untouched. He was the only truly human being in that room.

The Governor had shamed us and we tried to pass that on, and we failed. We were horrible. Ugly. Grotesque. We could not diminish him. We were hideous, diminished, small in our own eyes. He was steady, steadily human. He smiled at our silliness.

It got worse actually. I don't even want to think about it. I don't know what would have happened, but finally the officer from the crucifixion party came in to see what the delay was about. He laughed too, but awkwardly. Then someone handed the prisoner back his own tunic, sort of sheepish almost, and he pulled it over his head and said "thank you." Properly, nicely. I dismissed the battalion. It was over.

It was not right. Injustice at the top leads to shame at the bottom and shame leads to cruelty. But we did it ourselves. It has left me restless and uneasy.

I have a daughter back in Macedonia. She was nine when I last saw her, she'll be coming twelve now. She is so lovely: a skinny little thing, all legs and teeth, but lovely and I love her. And, perhaps because I'm not there enough, she loves me back. She loves her big, strong daddy, hero of the Empire, who marches away and comes back with gifts and laughter and joy. I might get home next year for a long leave if I'm lucky and she'll say, "What did you do in Jerusalem, Papa?" And what will I say? "I tortured a man about the same age as me; and it didn't work. I couldn't break him. He has broken me."

Back in barracks earlier, someone told me that the officer in charge of the crucifixion said afterwards that he thought the man was innocent; that he thought he was holy – "a Son of God", they say he said. But that doesn't feel right to me. He wasn't a god, not at all; he was just more human than anyone I have ever had to deal with before and I could not cope with it.

When I first saw this picture I couldn't look at it for too long. I thought it was scary and ugly and dark. I didn't like it at all. Now I still think all those things but I like it. It would have been a scary, ugly, dark time.

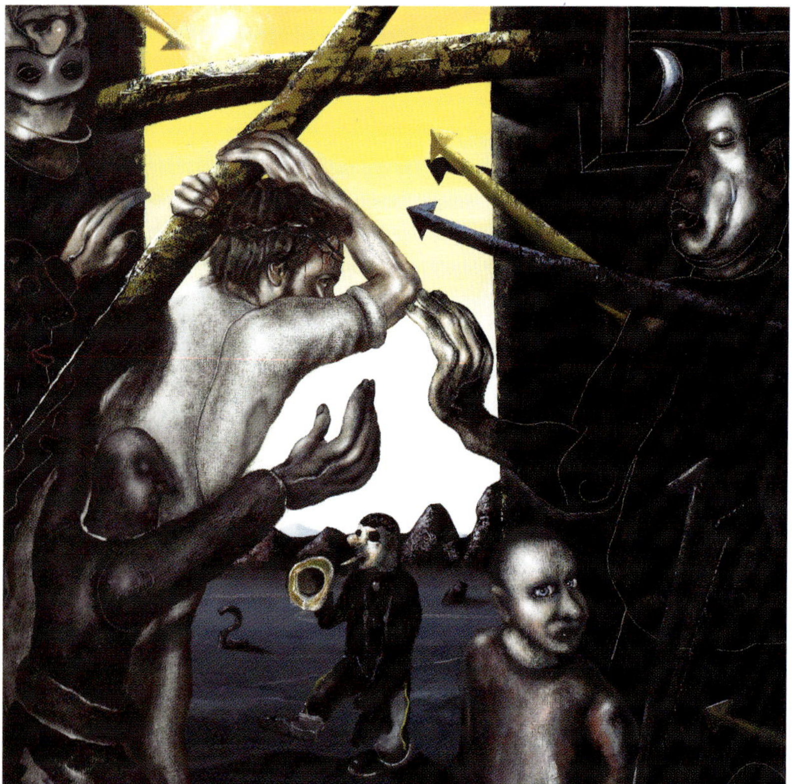

Station 2:
Jesus receives the Cross

They lead him out onto the parade ground, and the earth feels firm and cool under his bare feet. The trumpets sound, blaring and harsh, though not for him, and the walls do not come tumbling down, but he is out of the prison, out of the dark pit and in the warm morning sunlight. Briefly he feels a kind of joy, and under his breath he repeats his own words, "For this I was born, for this I have come into the world."

And "this" is not the pain and the dark of the night; "this" is not the anguished prayers in the garden or the pointless betrayals of friends. "This" is the sunshine and the morning; the fire flash of sun on polished bronze helmets, the restless pigeons rising against grey stone and blue sky; the elegant carriage of the young woman with a water vessel on her head; it is even the hard, healthy muscles of well-fed soldiers. "This," this is all joy and grace and morning.

As he is pushed beyond the shelter of the doorway he feels a little breeze and, although he knows it cannot be true because he is in the fetid, overcrowded city, miles south of Capernaum, he thinks he can smell the warmed grass and the heaved waves of spring flowers high on the hills above the Lake. He cannot help smiling for the pure delight of it; for the sweetness of those years of laughter and freedom. Joy is the fortress, the city of God – joy, and laughter, and wine, and song; joy is the house built on a rock. The rest hardly mattered. Freedom mattered; freedom and love and laughter.

They had called them "the spaces in between". They would be somewhere working, preaching, healing and talking, talking, talking; three days later they would be somewhere else, working, preaching, healing and talking, talking, talking. And in between were "the spaces in between."

What filled the spaces? High skies, as blue as heaven, with soft bands of mist on the lake below at dawn and dusk. The vast flocks of birds going determinedly south before the autumn rains and eagerly north after the spring rains, filling the air with a tremulous energy, a throbbing beat, even at night. The long, golden sweep of the high hill country – gaudy with flowers as the sun strengthened, and wide, tanned gold through the dry summer. Walking all day, and singing as they walked; singing the old songs in their own country. Hot afternoons, when they would come to small, leaping streams and splash and play like children. Huge stars at night, when they gathered round a little laughing fire, and talked, and talked, and talked.

Freedom and hope make love and laughter. Love and laughter create freedom and hope. In love they forgive each other; in laughter they begin to forgive themselves. This is the Kingdom, this is the sheepfold and the well that will not run dry. Here, now, louder than the clash of arms and the stamping of well-trained military feet, he hears and smiles at the high trill of girlish laughter when Mary of Magdala pulls off her headscarf, shakes out that extraordinary copper-coloured hair and laughs at herself for thinking she ever had to take to selling what could be given in freedom; and forgiving the men who abused her because she has forgiven herself. Or Matthew's bellow of ironic laughter that he had ever been so stupid as to believe that money stolen from the oppressed at the command of the oppressor was ever likely to be fun to spend. And other, deeper, heartaches, and sins, and follies, and limitations and pains, muttered in the dark; heard with tenderness, with recognition and then with love, acceptance and laughter.

The spaces in between were the places where freedom grew, as it had grown for their ancestors in the desert: freedom, and hope, and strength. And laughter.

He pauses. Ignores the sharp pain of the iron collar against his bruised neck. Never too late to learn he thinks wryly. It was the laughter that had undone them in the end. He knows that now. Prophets and preachers, even healers, were meant to be solemn and gloomy; doom-laden, accusatory; not singing and dancing. They had laughed too much, too loudly and with too little respect. It was baffling to him suddenly that people chose misery, liked misery, preferred misery to responsibility; loved to feel guilty but refused to feel forgiven. Refused to be free. Like their ancestors in the desert. He feels sad himself now: it is all a waste. Grab the chance, he wants to tell them, take a risk; but they will not. John came to them fasting, and they said he was mad; he came to them eating and drinking and laughing, and they said he was debauched. What tight-arsed, middle-of-the-road saviour do they want, if they want one neither fierce nor laughing?

The tug on the chain is more insistent. It calls him back to the present and he follows his guard across the parade-ground to where the crosses are waiting, stacked against the wall. He is still smiling, the memories slipping sideways and his own delight not following them quite fast enough, but left stranded in a foolish grin stuck slightly sideways on his face. He laughs aloud and sees the young soldier beside him jerk his head round, startled.

He notices that the whole manoeuvre has been surprisingly well timed. He and his two soldiers arrive where a pile of crosses is stacked up against a corner of the wall at almost the same moment as the two other similar little parties do. He will not have to do this thing alone. He looks at the other two and then at the crosses and cannot suppress a wave of nausea, welling in his throat, making his mouth taste bitter. Some of them are new, the bare wood still pale from the rough planing, but the others have been used before: the holes where the nails had been last time are dark scars on the surface stained with dry blood. He hopes they will give him a new one and then is surprised that he should think it matters any more. There are no more decisions to be made; now he has only to carry the cross up through the city to the hill and let them do what they will. The spirit is willing but his body still rejects the whole idea; he does not want to die like this; he does not want to die.

"I have come that you may have life, life in all its abundance."

"Anyone who believes in me will never die."

"I am the way, the truth and the life."

"Martha, I am the resurrection and the life. Can you believe this?"

Can he? Suddenly he is not quite sure that he can. Then he thinks of Martha and her little, chubby, weary legs running up the hill outside Bethany to throw herself into his arms. The thought of Martha, bossy, bustling, busy, would give anyone confidence. "Oh, my dear," she had said, "I believe you are the Christ, the one who is coming into the world." If he cannot quite believe it for himself this morning, he will believe it for her, for all of them.

The soldiers turn him round so he does not see which cross he gets. When it falls suddenly onto his shoulder it catches at one of the long, bloody furrows that the whips made and he almost cries out with the pain. He puts up his arms to shift and steady it and that drives the thorns of his crown deeper into his head. He reels, giddy, weak, sick with pain. "Abba" he cries out silently, "Abba, Father."

Perhaps it is the smell of the wood, perhaps it is all the times from childhood that he carried heavy planks from the shed to the workshop in Nazareth, perhaps it is the sunshine, perhaps it the sweet humility of God, but when his heart cries Abba his memory does not give him the power and strength of the God of Israel, El Shaddai, the Almighty, the God who travels with him. Instead, with a bright clarity he sees his other father, the carpenter, with his strong, clever hands, his infinite patience and his profound, calm detachment. Joseph. His memory smiles.

When he was younger he used to resent that detachment. His father loved his mother absolutely, generously and above all things; you could see it in every movement and moment they were together. And, as his father loved his mother, so his mother loved her son – and Joseph never moved to claim her back, or to claim him. He never quite knew what, if anything, it was that he had stolen from Joseph. But he had grown up, he knows now, now in this sunny compound, understanding that the ways of love are complex; twisted and twined around desire, around faith, and hope, and pity, and praise. Around passion and freedom. Now he needs that profound, calm love because he has to lug this cross out through the gate, up through the city, and onto the little hill where they are waiting for him.

He shifts the cross awkwardly on his bleeding shoulder and Joseph reaches out and balances it for him. "Go with the grain," he says as he said over and over again, leaning over the bench and covering the boy's hands with his own skilful, knowledgeable ones. "You're not a warrior with an enemy, you're a carpenter with a piece of wood. You're on the same team. Let it tell you. Go with the grain." He had known, early and certainly, that he would never be as good a carpenter as his father was. Now he knows he will never be as good a father either. Each to their own. Go with the grain. The cross feels more stable, though still too heavy, and he looks up and around.

The soldiers are now busy doing soldier things. They are forming a procession, a line of march, with the prisoners in the middle. Everyone knows that the streets are too narrow and the crowds will be too dense and pressing, so this beautiful, orderly column will collapse into a mild confusion of jostling and shoving before they have gone quarter of a mile, but still they form up with obvious pleasure.

It is warm in the sunshine; there is a small sweet breeze; the wood is rough and fresh-smelling against his cheek. Briefly, a bolder pigeon settles back onto the parade ground. There is an elegant grace in the hard, healthy muscles of the four well-fed soldiers who are pulling back the great bolts and swinging open the barracks gates; there is a low murmur from the crowd outside, like a wind rising across the lake.

"Company, tn-shun!"

There is a sharp clatter, a brisk stomp and then a moment of stillness.

This is the space in between, he thinks. Between the long, hideous night, when he had to pay perfect attention to too many things, and the long, hideous day ahead. This is a place of freedom. It is out of his hands now. Go with the grain. Not a warrior with an enemy, but a carpenter with a piece of wood. This is love and freedom and, if there is no laughter here, it was laughter that had brought him here.

"Company, by the left, forward march."

They make me think about Abu Graib; about that horrible prancing woman. Why would she do that and she was pregnant? Jesus was tortured. It wasn't just her; it was the war and everything. Now I feel sorry for her as well as the people who are tortured.

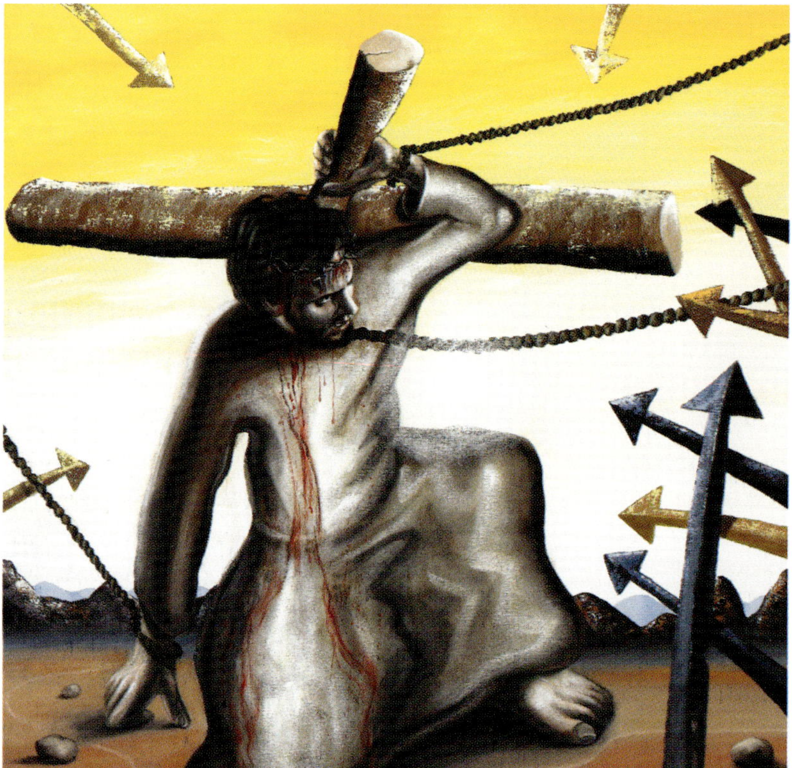

Station 3:
Jesus falls for the first time

They go out through the gates into the sullen city. The crowd is thick around the barracks and the soldiers have to push the people back, squeezing them against the walls. There is a half-hearted cheer as the prisoners emerge. He feels sorry for them, caught between the Hosannas of last week and the baying, howling mob of this morning; they are uncertain what they are cheering about. He feels some sympathy with their confusion, because they do not want to see themselves cheering the soldiers and he can understand that. In the final count he would rather be stoned by his own people than crucified by the imperial masters. But, when he had the chance, he turned it down; slipped away through the mob and went about his own business. Had he wanted to spare them the final guilt? If so, he had been wrong – they are going to kill him anyway, and he has shamed them. He has forced them to ask the occupying army, their conquerors, to do their dirty work for them. He is sorry about that now. Now he feels only compassion and a wry awareness that, no matter what he had done, it would have ended up here one way or another. Stoning feels preferable when you are on your way to crucifixion, but in all likelihood the reverse would prove true too.

And they did not want to cheer two robbers and a blasphemer. They did not know what they wanted, they were like a clutch of chickens running round looking for their mother; he wanted to gather them in and they did not want that. There is nothing he can do now, because they don't know what they want. If he is craven and penitent, they will hate him for not acting like a king; and if he acts like a king they will hate him because he is too proud. If they had liked him last week, humble and riding on a donkey, they should like him more now – humbler yet, even to accepting death on a cross – but it didn't work like that. There is shame in all their hearts, whatever they think of him, because in a dark moment, stirred up by the authorities and over-excited by Passover, they had called Caesar "King". They have seen themselves colonised and defeated, and they cannot forgive him for that. In their muddled half cheers and occasional boos they seem like children, like sheep without a shepherd, and he loves them, suddenly and fiercely. For himself, he is glad to be out of the pit, out in the city, under crowd law, which is crude but real, and beyond Roman law which is sophisticated and bogus.

Now it is all done, he thinks; it's all over. No more choices, no more effort, just accept it and let them all do what they had to do. There is a rhythm he can settle into and now he has found a comfortable balance for the cross which, although it is heavy, feels warm and somehow friendly against his cheek. He can do this, he thinks; he can do it.

For a few moments he is at peace. He loves these people. He loves this city. Once, years ago, when he was a little boy, he had run away to be here; he can see himself , slipping away from the caravan, scampering up the hill, delighted by his rare freedom, by his sense of adventure and by the bustling, busy, holy city, full of people and noise and talk and energy. Now he has come back, probably no wiser than he was then. He is in the right place and at the right time. Jerusalem is his city; Passover is his feast. He has got it right. God is good to him. He can do this.

And then, as the procession makes a sharp left-hand turn, he sees the temple, far away and high above the street with the sun behind it, and he is distracted, or the cross-beam catches on something, or something . . . and he stumbles, struggles for his balance and crashes his knee painfully against a cobble stone. Someone in the crowd laughs, and there is Satan, close and grinning.

"'Turn back, dear soul, to your rest, for the Lord has been good: he has kept your soul from death, your eyes from tears and your feet from stumbling.' If you are the Son of God, of course."

"No," he says, "no. Go away."

"I don't see why I should," says Satan, "this seems to me a very opportune moment, a convenient time."

"Last night," he mutters, as the soldiers pull him back up onto his feet. The whole black weight of last night – his sleeping friends, and his desperate desire to escape, to live, to laugh – presses down on him again; and the edge of the cross finds an open wound in his shoulder and he flinches.

"Last night was your chance. That's enough."

"Says who? No – last night was fun, but you know how it was: the flesh was weak but the spirit was willing. Now the flesh is even weaker and I am wondering about the spirit. Of course, if you had turned the stones into bread as I suggested, you wouldn't be here, and they wouldn't be hurting your poor knee. But, you know, you can still get out of this if you want."

"The Lord is my shepherd; there is nothing I can want."

But it did not sound entirely convincing. He seeks for the quiet, inner place where he talks to his Father, but it is hard to pray when the army of occupation is tugging on your leash as though you were an ill-bred puppy; when the great stripes of blood across your back are beginning to make your tunic stick and rip with each step; when the heavy weight of a cross strong enough to hold you up until you are dead is pressing into your shoulder; when, each time you move your head, a thorn sharper than the serpent's tongue wriggles against the bone of your forehead; when your knee hurts like a little child's; when your so-called friends are conspicuous by their absence; and when a foolish crowd is sniggering at you.

"Are you sure?" asks Satan blandly. "Nothing? Well of course he will never allow you to stumble; and he's not going to let the sun smite you when you are hanging up there at noon. He's guarding your going out and your coming in, isn't he? Look, get real: he is not even guarding your soul, because he's letting me be here. Are you sure your Abba-daddy is up to the job? Are you sure he loves you? No-one else seems to."

It is too much; he is too tired. He wants to stop the whole thing right here, to take a break, go up in the hills and pray; up there where he can concentrate, remember the good times, pray through the night, find and feel the connection, while the huge stars sing to him silently. Then he can come back, can come back and begin again and get it right this time. He must pray more. Pray and praise. Abba, Father.

The tug on the rope is impatient, insistent. He is back on his feet, but reeling. Pray, he thinks. Pray. Abba, Father. Pray, prey, play, pay – the words begin to run together and Satan smiles.

He is too tired. It has been too much. He has not slept all night, and before that there was the terror in the garden – the long dark hours when he had not thought he could go on; when he could not feel the connection, when he had been alone. And before that . . . and before that. Less than two weeks ago they had been across the Jordan in the wilderness, sunny and calm. They had escaped, got away . . . or had they run away? How do you tell? How do you ever know why you do what you do, why you did what you did? The consequence of freedom is responsibility – perhaps it is easier to be driven like lambs to the slaughterhouse without choice, at the mercy of events and things, without freedom. If you are free, you have to choose; and you have to choose without knowing. He had chosen less than a month ago to leave Jerusalem, to slip away quietly by night and take to the hills. He was not ready; they were not ready. And would they ever be? He had chosen to go and then, two weeks ago, he had chosen to come back. Or not chosen. Are the requirements of love freely chosen? Ever? He came back because he loves Martha and Mary and Lazarus. Because

Martha had sent for him, knowing what it meant and calling him nonetheless. If he did not come back for love, but only to prove that he could indeed raise the dead there was not any point to it, to any of it, but if he came back because she called to him, because she needed him and wanted him, then did he come freely, had he chosen? Was he free? And if love binds you rather than frees you, then in loving them all he is binding them and he wants to set them free. He had told the others that they were free, that they did not have to come back to Bethany with him – and he had seen their irritation. "We may as well come and die with you," Thomas had said, baffled, annoyed. Peter had said much the same thing a couple of years ago when he had suggested that they left him. "Oh yeah! And where could we go? We will never be free of you – you have the message of eternal life." Peter had known, Peter had always known, but, but even so . . . he cannot think about Peter now. Peter, Judas, and who else?

He is too tired to work it out. Love and freedom, justice and mercy, truth and peace. It is all too difficult. He just has to carry this heavy cross along this crowded road because he has freely chosen to move beyond choice.

But Satan whispers in his ear that he still has choices. He can make it stop.

"If you are the Son of God," Satan murmurs, "you can turn these stones into bread for the people; not just for you now, but for all these people you say you love. You can raise up new children for Abraham, here in the Holy City; you can pull the pillars of the Empire down upon these heathen heads; you can set them all free."

And, after he raised Lazarus, he had dithered. They went to Jerusalem; they went back to Bethany; he led them all down to Ephraim, on the very edge of the wilderness and he had looked out at the hot, silent emptiness. Was he running away? Was he protecting them? Could they have gone out into the wilderness like John? Should they be like the Essenes, pure and rigorous and holy? They went back to Jerusalem. He was looking for a way to do it. He lost his temper – he smashed up the temple market, he preached those enormous condemnatory sermons and the crowd loved it; but they loved the risk of it too. Dangerous, heady stuff. So they went back to Bethany. He had dithered, waiting for a sign. And the sign was Passover. As king he came into his city, humbly riding on a donkey.

"Show-off," says Satan. "Good theatre, but a bit foolish. Burned your boats didn't you?"

Had he meant to? Is he still showing off?

"Waste of time, you know; waste of a great opportunity."

"No," he says, aloud this time.

One of the soldiers looks round. "Are you ready then? Come on, we haven't got all day."

"Go away," he says to Satan, "Go away. I'm too busy. I've got a long day ahead of me. The spirit is willing."

"You wait," says Satan and he sniggers. "You wait."

Once I fell over in the street and what I felt was really embarrassed, so I shouldn't be glad to see him like this – but I am.

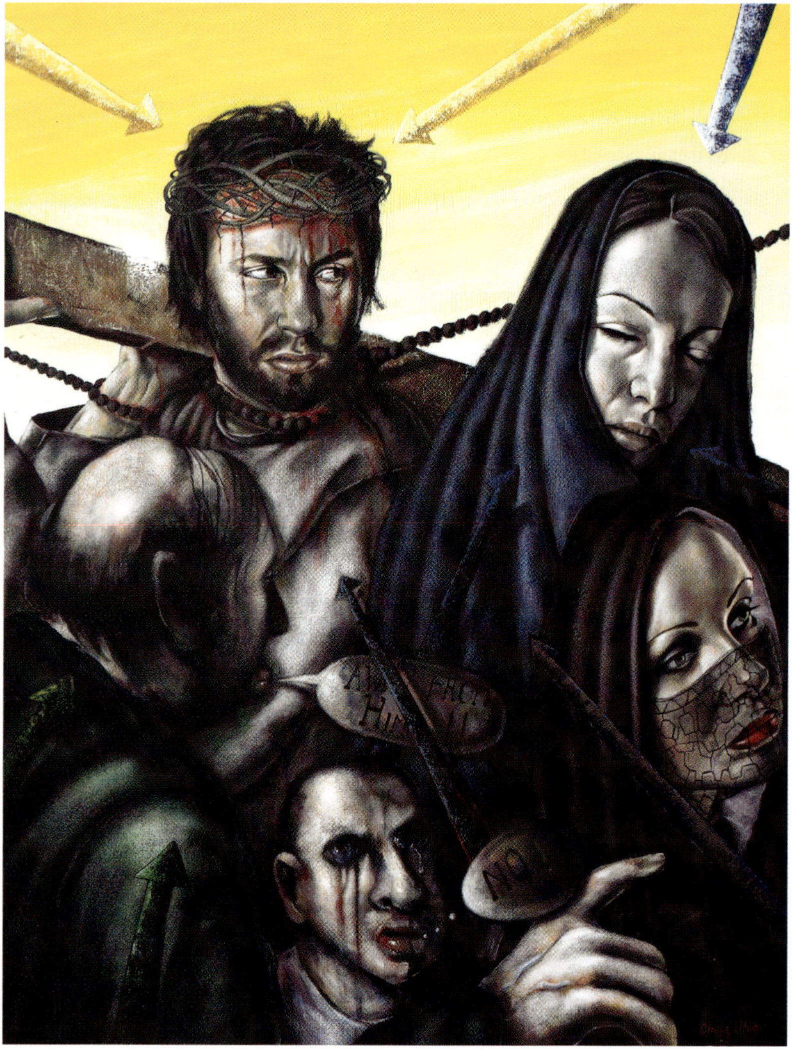

Station 4: Jesus meets his mother

After the meal, I was so tired that I did not go out with them to the Garden. I wasn't sure where they would all be sleeping tonight; whether they would go out to Bethany again, or come back to the house, or go somewhere else. I did not want to walk alone through the city, and I was briefly uncertain about what to do. As I get older, I find this lack of planning increasingly difficult. But our kind hostess showed me to the women's quarters, shook out a bedroll for me and left me in peace. I was not sure that I would sleep. Jerusalem at this time of year is noisy, even after dark; but it wasn't the noise that I thought would keep me awake, it was the anxiety and the tension.

I came down from Galilee with the Nazareth pilgrims, as I have done almost every year of my life, walking the well-known and much-loved road and singing the great pilgrimage songs:

> On the holy mountain is the city he founded,
> The Lord loves the gates of Zion
> More than all the dwelling places of Jacob.
> Glorious things are spoken of you, City of God.
>
> I was glad when they said to me,
> Let us go up to the house of the Lord.

But naturally I hoped I would see him. I was pretty certain he too would be in the City for the Passover. Jerusalem is his city; Passover is his time. That has always been true. Of course he would want to be in Jerusalem for Passover, and of course it is my fault that he wants this because, when he was growing up, we always made the journey – every single year. I insisted on it.

These last months have been the longest time that I have gone without seeing him since he was born. I was eager and hopeful. And indeed, within less than twenty-four hours of arriving in the City I found him preaching in the Temple and arguing with the Pharisees – twenty-four hours was a good deal shorter than the first time I had looked for him in Jerusalem and found him arguing with the Pharisees. That thought made me smile. His obvious pleasure in seeing me made me smile too, and so did the welcome I got from his friends. But quite quickly I became aware that, this year, something has shifted; time seems to have speeded up; there is a sort of throbbing and volatile excitement in them all, and it makes me nervous.

There was a new anger in his preaching, but also a deep, yearning sorrow. I began, with a kind of horror, to believe that he had gone too far and that they would try to kill him. I began to believe that he knew this too; and yet he was being so provocative, so outspoken, so – it felt to me – foolhardy, that I wanted to talk to him about it, to warn him, perhaps; to know what he was feeling, what he was planning. I held my peace. When he was twelve years old, he had made it painfully clear to me that what he did in Jerusalem had nothing to do with me. Yesterday morning I woke up from a dream about Elizabeth, and what I felt was envy – she had been dead and buried before the head of her son had been carried by that wanton girl round the hall of Herod's palace. I knew I was not going to be so lucky.

But then it was a lovely day, yesterday. The city felt vibrant – alive and exciting. Of course there were crowds and noise and the continual aggressive presence of the Roman soldiers; but it was feast time, and festival, and the sun was shining, and I thought perhaps I was being foolish, over-concerned. The only thing I really had to give him any more was my confident serenity. I was the one person who knew fully who and what he was, and I had to hold on to that for him.

Around midday, I met Simon Peter and Andrew coming up towards the Temple, looking cheerful and energetic. They were clearly pleased to see me; they had been coming to look for me, they said, because they now had a place for the Passover meal and they all wanted me with them. I was so pleased.

"Did he say so?" I asked.

It is so hard for a mother not to put herself first with her child. Not to feel that, because she has known him longest, she also knows him best. We come to feel this way when they are small because, when they are small, it is true; but it is hard to give it up – to accept that an adult child has a whole life, has friends and people and work that you do not know about and never will; that are not your business and shouldn't be; and that love means not making those demands, but giving a child its own freedom. I had had to learn this and he taught me. "Who is my mother?" he said, out loud, in public. He did not even invite me in but, they say, he stretched out his hand to his friends and told the crowd, "Here, look: these are my mother and my family." It hurt. I learned.

So I asked, "Did he say so?"

They were clear that he had. He had asked Andrew to go down to the caravanserai that the Nazareth group were using and leave a message for me, that they had all been told to invite me if they met me.

It was a strange but lovely evening. The tension had not dissolved; there was a dark current of anxiety pulling at us all, but the ritual of the meal channelled it, in the way good ritual does. He held the whole room – the meal, the old pieces of the Passover ceremonies and the new pieces that he gave us; he held them for us all with so much grace and intelligence and artistry. And somehow, during the evening, I was given a gift. A question that has haunted me since before he was born was answered deep in my heart. Ever since the morning when the angel came and changed my life forever, I had wondered, "Why me?"

and now I knew. It was simple. Any moderately devout woman could have taught him the traditions and the songs and the laws, but he had needed a sense of the deep patterns; a grace of hand and eye, a feeling for timing and meaning. There was hope and faith and truth – but they needed shaping into ritual and beauty and love. That is what I had given him, almost without knowing it. My soul magnified the Lord, and my spirit rejoiced in God my saviour.

But, after the meal, I was so tired that I did not go out with them to the Garden. I went to bed and, perhaps unexpectedly, fell asleep.

In the darkest part of the night, I was woken suddenly. There was a banging on the street door, and someone shouting to be let in. Somebody had obviously not gone to bed, because almost immediately I heard the bolts being pulled back. There was a quick babble of voices that I could not hear clearly, then a loud cry of pain or anger. I lay still. It was fully dark in the room and I did not know this house, or its owners. Almost I thought I would turn over and go back to sleep. Eventually there was a sound outside the doorway, and someone said, "Mary," very quietly.

"Yes. I'm awake."

A woman came in with a lamp. She was crying. She said, "They've arrested him."

I did not need to ask who. I had a bright golden image of him, perhaps about eight years old, running down the street towards me in the last of the sunlight. I am watching him, with my arms out to welcome him home, and laughing and thinking there is no greater joy than this – to have your son run into your arms and let you hold him. And he will be called Emmanuel, which means God with us.

Then the image wavered and was gone. I struggled to get up. I felt so old and so tired.

In the courtyard there was confusion and grief and muddle. No one knew what was happening. No one knew where he was. They had taken him to the Sanhedrin. No, they had taken him to Herod. No, they had taken him to the Romans. They had killed him. They were going to kill him. They could not kill him, because the Romans would not let them. They had flogged him. He had escaped. They were trying him. We did not know; we did not know anything. The householder took a servant and went to find out. He did not come back. John came; he was looking for Peter and would not say why. People came and went, and we could not find out anything for certain. People were kind to me. I tried to hold on to pictures of him – the image of him running up the street, the image of him as a tiny baby sleeping in my arms, the image of him breaking the bread for us only a few hours ago; and I could not. I tried to hold the angel's voice in my head against the babble of ignorance and fear; and I could not.

Gradually it grew light. Gradually we found out. They had arrested him in the garden last night; they had taken him to the Sanhedrin who had found him guilty, although no one seemed to know what he had been accused of. They were seeking the death penalty, so they had sent him to the Roman Governor. He was being tried there.

People came and went, but it all seemed strangely silent. Then, in the silence, there was an extraordinary sound – like a wind or a dark drumbeat, but human. It rose and fell, a throbbing roar. "It's the crowd," someone said. And, eventually, we heard what they were roaring. We were all very still, frozen. A bit later things started to speed up again. Pilate condemned him. He was sentenced to death by crucifixion. They were going to do it today, this morning. Now.

Suddenly, I had to see him. I had to. I slipped out of the courtyard, unnoticed. It was easy to find out where he was from the sound of the crowd, and I pushed and shoved my way through the people. I wanted to shout "Let me through, let me through, I'm his mother," but I could not, because of his cool clarity: Who is my mother? He would not let me say it. I had learned well.

So I came to a corner, just part of the crowd; and I could hear he was not far away and was coming towards me. I thought I could stand

and wait and, when he came up to me, I would rush out, hold him, kiss him, weep in his arms. I had to.

But I did not. I saw him before he saw me. I saw that he was tired, even more tired than I was. I saw that he was hurt; there was blood on his face and the cross was heavy. He was completely alone, despite the crowd. He was holding himself together with a real effort. I think he was trying to talk to God... I think so – it is hard to tell. I saw that the last thing he needed was a weeping mother. He had his work to do. I felt as though someone had driven a sword into my guts, and my heart was broken.

Our eyes met, but I did not wait to read his expression. I turned away.

"Who is my mother?" he had asked, and he had answered his own question, "She who hears my words and keeps them." It was the least I could do.

Later I thought that I could hold him and kiss him and weep over him after he was dead, when I would not get in his way or in the way of his friends. So, in the afternoon, I walked up the road to the place where my son was dying.

I don't understand this very well; I don't understand their expressions. What I feel is that they are both so strong, and their relationship is very strong too, whatever it is. I like to look at this and try and understand.

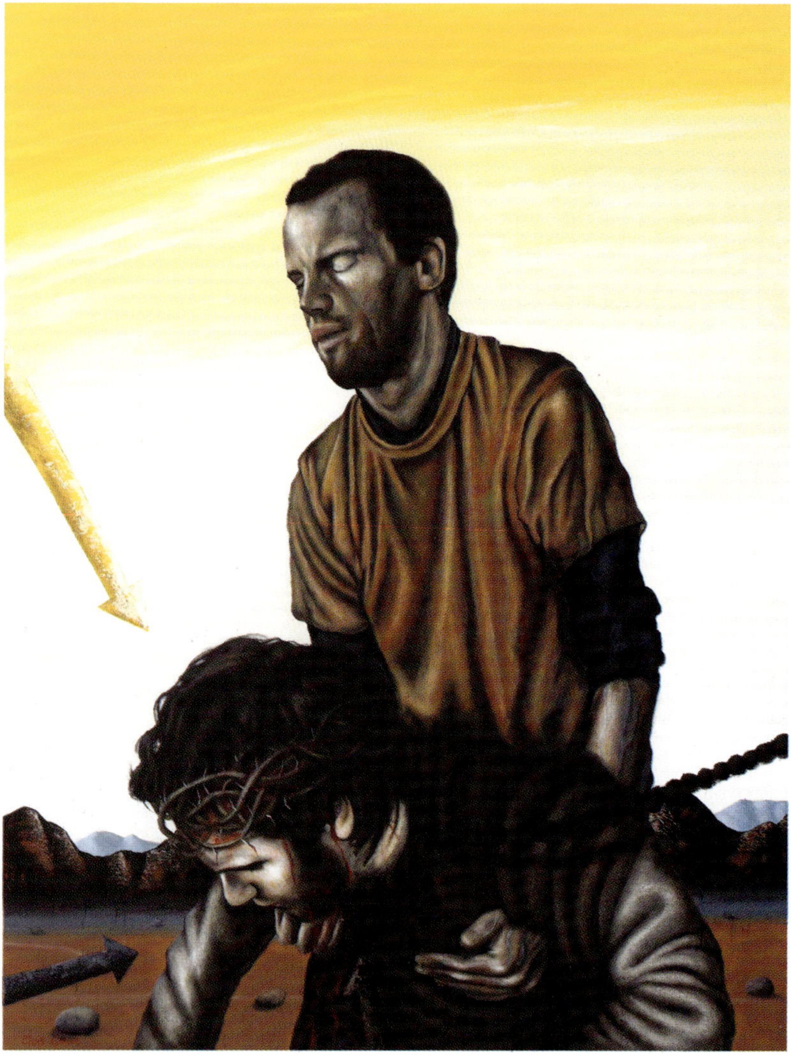

Station 5:
Simon of Cyrene carries the Cross

I'm not really a man for telling stories, so you'll have to bear with me. I'll probably tell this all wrong.

One thing I never quite know is where you are supposed to start a story. I mean, if you just say, "We got up in the morning," or "When we got to Jerusalem," or something like that, no one's who's listening – if anyone is listening – knows what you are on about. They don't know who the "we" is for one thing, never mind all the other things. And anyway, I don't think it did begin that morning, or when we got to Jerusalem.

If I really try to tell it from the beginning, then it probably began when she and the little girl died. I know you are supposed to want boys, but we had two boys and she really wanted a girl this time; to be honest, I did too. She was fine right up through the pregnancy and there had been no problem with the boys, so I don't know what happened. She just died – her and the baby. But you see I can't even say it begins there, because if I hadn't loved her, if the boys hadn't loved her, if we hadn't been married and had the boys, if she hadn't been so lovely and made me so happy then things wouldn't have changed when she died; so that isn't the beginning either.

So, to cut a long story short we – and that means me and my two boys, Rufus and Alexander (and don't tell me those aren't Jewish names, that's a long story and I'm not telling it now) – we got up in the morning, and when we got to Jerusalem the whole city was in turmoil.

No, wait. I knew this would happen: I've hardly started and I need to interrupt myself to explain something, and this is important. I am not the sort of bloke who takes his little boys to watch a crucifixion; that is just not my scene. I know there are men who think it is good for their sons to see it and learn, to understand about justice and righteousness, but I've seen a couple myself and, quite frankly, No. And especially not my two, all shaken up and sad and fretful because of her dying. Even without that, though, I don't really get it, because crucifixion is a Roman thing and I can't see how they are going to get much about justice and righteousness out of watching a bunch of pagan invaders banging up some of our own. But one thing I have learned in the last sorry months is how hard it is to bring up children in a way that pleases you, never mind trying to please other people, so I wouldn't say this to anyone else – they have to make up their own minds about things like that. And if you think I'm having a go here, you're right: I can't believe how many people tell me the boys should be with their grandmother, without knowing the first thing about it. Well, her mother's dead and no one who wasn't demented would leave a dog with my mother. Even my sister knows that, and she does help out all she can, but in the end it's mine to deal with and I do my best.

So, where was I? We got up in the morning and when we got to Jerusalem the city was in turmoil. We hadn't gone to see the crucifixion; in fact I hadn't even known there was a crucifixion going on. We'd gone because we all needed a bit of a break. I thought I'd take the boys and show them the Temple, and maybe, if I got the mood right, we'd say a prayer for her – with children you have to careful about those sorts of things, and they are the sort of things I am not very good at being careful about, but she was, and so I have to try. Then I thought it would be fun for them to see the crowds and sing the songs with them, and get something to eat and maybe buy them some fairings. Just a day out, and allowed because of the religious angle.

It turned out not to be such a brilliant idea, which shouldn't have surprised me, I suppose. Something else I should have told you is that

I am tall: I'm a big, tall, hefty bloke and I had forgotten that being in a big crowd when you are tall is quite different from being in a big crowd when you are six or eight. Down there it is scary: you can't see anything and you feel you are going to get trampled on and pushed around. So I put Rufus up on my shoulders which is fine, but Alexander's whining and clinging like he does too often now, so I decide we'll leave the Temple and go down into the city and try and find a bit more open space. So we cut down from the Temple mound and head north a bit, and it is all much easier and we are getting a bit more comfortable and happier all round when we find ourselves in another crowd; and there are soldiers pushing us all about, and there is something ragged and nasty going on. But we can't turn round and get out because there are too many people. I back us up against a wall and there are these two old women beside me and I ask them what's happening and one of them says, "They're going to crucify him". She looks up at me and I see she's blubbing. I don't know what I would have said, but now Alexander is working himself up into a real state. So I have to swing Rufus off my shoulders so I can hold Alexander.

Then there is more pushing and shoving and general chaos, and some stupid Roman officer on a horse is coming down the street, clearing a way for himself with his whip. He stops just beside us and calls above the crowd,

"What's the delay here, men? Come on, hurry it up."

And then someone shouts back about the guys falling over and the crosses are too heavy or something, and the officer glowers a moment and then he looks round and before I know what's happening he looks straight at me.

"You," he barks, "You get out here and help carry a cross."

I start to say about the boys, but I feel a sharp sting like a bee on my ear and it's his whip. Alexander starts screaming and Rufus is snivelling and I really, really do not want them to have to see their father being whipped and humiliated, nor them having to follow behind him and then watch some Roman bastard thumping nails into some guy's hands; and this was only meant to be a little holiday for us, to cheer us up. I can see her, laughing at me, but nicely and making everything all right; holding Rufus and comforting Alexander, and she isn't here, and I can't bear it. I'm panicking a bit myself because I just don't know what to do, and the whip comes again, catching me across the face and drawing blood.

"We'll take the boys," says a quick voice. "You won't want them to see this."

"Oh Martha," says the other woman.

"Sorry," says the first one, "I mean, I'll take the boys. There's a wine shop, with a garden, down below the barracks – The Camel, it's called. I'll take them there." She looks at the other one, "You go on. It's all right – he'll want you there."

The whip comes again, and another sharp order. I don't have much choice. Then something weird happens. Alexander gulps and says in a funny little meant-to-be-grown-up voice, "Go on, Da, we'll be OK." And he smiles at this woman. He never smiles any more, not out of the house. But he smiles at her and she smiles back. I don't want him to see the blood, and I don't want to catch the thong again.

"Yes, Sir," I say to the officer, and push away from the wall to stand at his spur until the crowd parts and the victims come through, in chains, hauling these ridiculous planks along with them.

So I get assigned to the first bloke. I'm a good bit heftier than he is, and a lot taller; I could probably carry the whole thing myself easier than the two of us together, but he's going to die in a pretty horrible way later so I don't want to shame him, and we sort of yoke together like oxen, with the leg of the cross between us. He knows I'm taking more than my share though, even if other people can't see it, and after a little while he says, "Thank you".

Now one thing I've often noticed is that men find it really hard to be grateful to someone who does a physical job for them that they can't do themselves, so I was a bit surprised that he said thank you so sweetly. He meant it. I turn my head, awkwardly really, and look at him and he smiles at me. And I find myself smiling back, just like Alexander did at the woman. There is something about his smile that made me . . . well, like Alexander I haven't done much smiling recently, and it felt good.

Something strange happened to me on that road. He was really tired, you could see that, and stressed out. Sometimes he was weaving about as though he was drunk, but I don't think he was. Twice he actually fell, heavily, and once I went over with him and it hurt; the cross pinned us down and he was lying with his face in the ground and the soldiers had to come and lift the cross off us so we could stand, and even then I had to help him up. By the end I had my arm round him, trying to help, trying to support him. Sometimes he stopped and stood still, seemed to go away inside himself, and a couple of times he talked to people in the crowd; but the rest of the time, even when he was reeling, he talked to me – or really he let me talk to him.

I'm not going to tell you all about it, partly because it was personal and partly because it doesn't really have anything to do with the story; but here is this man, so tired I could feel it seeping out of him, bleeding all over the place, knowing what was going to happen next and not liking it, and still he paid attention to me. It might have felt weird, you know: here I was, arm in arm with another guy, holding him, hugging him, and talking to him about all my own stuff – about her, and her dying, and the boys, and how it all worried me; and how Alexander had shut himself down and I didn't know how to get him to come back, and I had shut down too and didn't want to come back much. I even told him about my mother, and I don't do that, ever. But it didn't feel weird; it felt great. I've never talked like that to anyone except her.

Every now and again I'd remember where we were, and I'd get embarrassed and say I was sorry, that he had bigger things on his mind, and that sort of talk; but he'd just smile and say something and I'd be off again. And I'll tell you one more really weird thing: all the time we were walking up that hill I never once wondered what it was that he had done, why we were here.

So we arrive. There's a wee little pause while the soldiers get themselves sorted, and we dump the cross on the ground and just stand there. Then he says, as though it was just ordinary and I had given him a lift somewhere in my cart or something, "Well, you'd better get back to those boys. Can you give Martha a message from me? Say I said, 'thank you.' Tell her I said she chose rightly this time. She'll understand."

It was a bit tricky to know how to leave, but I did have to get back to the boys. I sort of fidgeted a bit. Then he said, "Look, it's not for me to tell you, but you might let her help with them." I was about to tell him I could manage now, but he smiled again and said quickly, "It's not for you – you'll cope fine; it's for her. She needs people to look after." He gives me a quick hug and then I can see he's going away from me and into himself. He wants to be alone. So I go.

I go down the town to look for The Camel, and suddenly I surprise myself. I hear me singing. I haven't sung since she died; I've helped a man to his death, and now I am singing. Strange day.

I find The Camel, like she said. It's a nice place; there are a couple of men drinking, and the landlord sees me and says, "She said you'd be along as soon as you could. She's out back with the children. Nice kids." He says it like we're old friends. I go through the room towards the back and there's a heavy leather curtain over the exit. I push it aside and I hear Alexander's voice, shrill, excited – joyful. "Look at me, Martha, look at me!"

I jump up onto the grassy patch and there is Martha, with Rufus asleep in her lap, just laughing and watching Alexander. He is turning a clumsy summersault, head over heels in the sunshine. "I can do that too," I call to him. And I do.

That's how I got to know them. That's the story.

He is carrying Jesus; not just the cross but Jesus himself. I like this picture so much – the idea that I can support Jesus as well as him supporting me. I wish I was able to do that more.

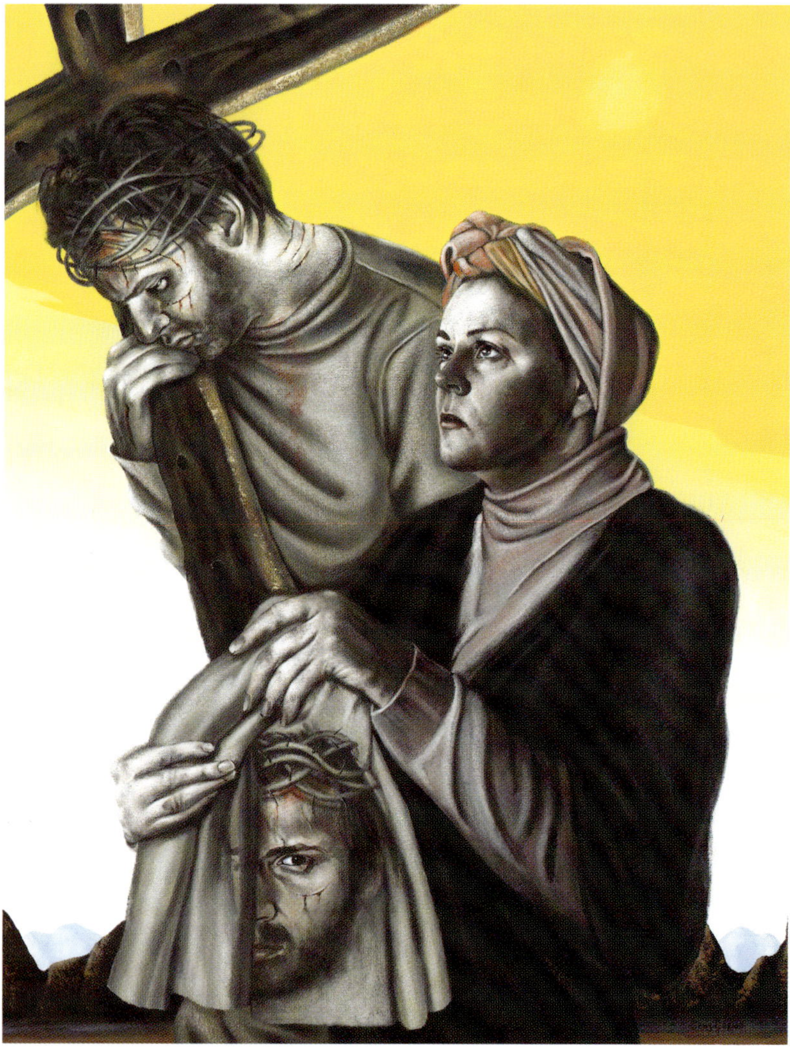

Station 6:
Veronica wipes Jesus' face

My heart stops. I am looking out from the roof at the crowd who are packed into the street below – avid, eager, greedy as people can be greedy for the shame of others. I may even have been thinking "some-one else's turn." I know that avid, prurient curiosity all too well.

I look down, casually, and my heart stops because I see that it is him. I do not want it to be him; I do not want to be called back into memory. This is my first visit to Jerusalem. I am free: I can go about in the crowd without having to take responsibility for their danger of contamination; I can walk freely in the Temple courtyards, visit with a friend, enjoy all the sites and the bustle and tension of the streets. I can praise God in his own house, and receive guests in mine. After twelve years, I am free; and I do not want to have to go back into the shame.

But it is him. I cannot help remembering. His shame and the mood of the crowd are too precise, too like mine; I cannot just put aside all those twelve years, and forget.

Wrapped in the bloody rags of my shame, exhausted by all the washing and the changing, embarrassed by the knowledge that my neighbours all knew, worn out by the curse on me, I had staggered up the crowded street in Capernaum just as he staggers up this one. He is bleeding; I was bleeding.

Each time I went down to the washing-place I could see the gos-sips eyeing me with a delicate and half-discreet curiosity, a kind of tender fearfulness. I hated it and I had to go; if I could have afforded to, I would have burned my soiled cloths and kept to the privacy of my own house, but untouchable, unmarriageable, defiled and defiling, always unclean, I had no access to money. Any that came, usually through my brother's weary charity and his wife's weary fear, I would spend on doctors who could hardly bear to touch me, who would blame me, and fear me, and who would not help me. The young married women turned aside in the road, not wanting to catch the contagion of ill-favour or bad luck. I frightened them; I exposed the fragility of the shapes that made their lives. They would hush their voices, kind but cruel.

Twelve years. Twelve years – four thousand, three hundred and eighty days. And each morning I would have to strip off the blood-stained linen cloths and wrap on clean ones. Each morning I would examine my conscience, carefully going through each space of time across my whole life to find out what I had done that I should be so punished. There was nothing there. I was innocent. I had not been one jot more sinful than other women who now had four or even seven sons. And, as I walked as privately as I could through each day, I could feel my rage growing heavy, sodden with loss; and my own body, daily less fed, less rounded and less beautiful. Bitterness flowed in to fill the spaces where the blood flowed out.

I don't remember now how I first heard of him, or even exactly what I heard. They were talking about a man who healed people – loonies, the demonic, lepers even. Anyone: you didn't seem to have to earn it, or join him, or anything. They said he was strange, that he hung out with the riff-raff, with hookers and tax collectors and – may I be forgiven – I thought, "Well, I'm not as bad as that." Then I thought, "It's worth a try." I'd reached the point where anything was worth a try.

After that I heard that he healed by touching. He would not touch me. I knew he would not touch me. He would ask me what healing I needed and I would have to tell him, and he would pull back, disgusted, and he would not touch me. Even if I did not tell him, someone would; they would move away from him and me, there would be a space around us. Some one would shout out a warning and he would step back, horrified, and I would be shamed. If he knew, he would not touch me. I didn't have the gall to ask him to touch me. I could not face the shame of him refusing to touch me.

But one morning I was standing in my doorway looking out at the lake. It was a pretty morning, with the lake all sparkling and bright. I love the lake, the great stretch of water that moves and shimmers in the sunlight, moody, vast and clean. I was just looking, and there was a boat, just an ordinary fishing boat and it was clearly putting in to our harbour. It wasn't a local boat, and it was surprisingly full of people. They were making an awkward job of tacking her in under sail in the light breeze. I was just watching, mindlessly, wearily. Then the street was full of people, pushing down to the waterfront – even in the press, they pulled back to avoid touching me, however accidentally. There was a sort of excitement, and finally I understood that it was him, the Teacher, and that they were coming ashore here. It was his boat I had seen, him and his friends coming back from the other side.

I could not let the chance go. I would not ask him to touch me, I would just touch him; touch a bit of his cloak or something. For the first time in years, I had what I recognised was hope. I was hopeful that he might heal me if I just touched the hem of his cloak.

It was terrible going out there into the crowd, being pressed against people and hoping all the time they wouldn't notice. The crowd was dense, I was not used to it; I had lived alone a long time. What kept me going was anger. Anger can give you courage; I was so angry at my whole, wasted, horrible life; at all these people who ignored me, and at God. Let them all be defiled, I thought; let them be contaminated, forced out, untouchable, unwanted. Let them feel what it's like. I was tired of being ashamed, I was tired of helping other people to make me ashamed in order to protect them from their shame. I was going to do what I had to do, and he could like it or lump it.

When I touched his long cloak the bleeding stopped. I knew in my body that I was healed.

But when he turned and asked who had touched him I wanted to die. I knew I should not have been there, defiling the whole community with the filth of my womanhood. I was frightened. I could not breathe, I could not think, panic strangled me. I started to sweat and to blush; a great tide of blood swept up through my whole body, the hotness and the redness of blood covering me all over as though it had broken through the cloths and would run out and contaminate the whole world. And he reached out and took me into his arms. He held me. No one had held me, or touched me, for twelve years. He held me close and gently, his arms wrapped firmly round me with my head against his shoulder, protecting me, covering my shame with his cloak. He held me.

When I touched his cloak, I knew in my body that I was healed. Women have talked to me about quickening, about the mysterious, beautiful moment when your child first moves deep in your belly – it was like that. When I touched the hem of his cloak, something mysterious and beautiful, deep in my belly, quickened and I knew that I was healed.

So now I look down from the roof, casually, and my heart stops because I see that it is him. He is reeling; the cross is heavy, and the soldiers are trying to humiliate him. The crowd, packed into the street below are avid, eager, greedy as people can be greedy for the shame of others. And suddenly I am angry. Anger can give you courage: I am so angry that I do not even think it through. He should not be made ashamed, and I will do what I have to do. They can like it or lump it.

I go down the steps and out onto the street, into the crowd. I want to give him something so at the doorway I pick up the jar of water, there for arriving guests. I will give him a drink, I think. I push through the crowd to get close to him as I pushed through it before.

The cavalcade has stopped for some reason and he is leaning on the cross, exhausted, his head hanging. I offer him a drink, and slowly he looks up, turns towards me, focuses; he has a look of mild curiosity as though he were struggling to see me, perhaps to remember where he has seen me before. But that does not matter. I feel slightly sick. Someone for some sick joke has rammed a sort of coronet of thorns on his head and it is bleeding. Someone has spat in his face. His hands are tied so he cannot wipe it; spit and blood and sweat and probably tears have clotted and dried so that he cannot see properly. He is so weary. He just stands there.

A drink is not enough. I take the hem of my veil and dip it in the water jar and start to wash his face, very carefully, very tenderly. After he healed me, after the seven days of waiting, after the satisfaction of the prying, dirty-minded Rabbi, I went to the mikvah and they washed me. Women with strong, tender, careful hands washed me. I had not been touched for twelve years, and the washing was so sweet and strong. I want to pass on to him all that sweetness and strength. He took away my uncleanness and I want to take away his. Despite the restless and uncomfortable crowd, who do not like this, despite the pushing of the soldiers who seem just to want to get on with the job, he and I stand together there in a peaceful, silent place and I wash his face. Not his mother or his lover: just a woman to whom he owes nothing, a woman without needs or demands, whose feelings he does not have to take care of – that woman washes his face.

And when it is done, when I have washed and dried that poor, broken face, I put my hand on his shoulder. I am planning to say some helpful, encouraging word, though I do not know what that would be. But, quite abruptly, he leans forward and drops his head into the hollow where my neck meets my shoulder, where his face is hidden from the crowd. One of the thorns from that evil, mocking circle pricks me, just below my ear. It hurts but I do not flinch; I am solid for him, and I suddenly feel his whole body relax against mine. I take the weight, and the sharp pain, and I know in my body that he is comforted.

Just a few seconds . . . and then the soldiers move in, rough and determined. They push me away, and he turns to his heavy work, and goes on up the hill.

I don't know if he recognised me. I doubt it, really. One woman in a crowd, over a year ago, a hundred miles north of here: I doubt it. But it doesn't matter. For one moment, his heavy forehead rested on my shoulder, and I knew in my body that he was consoled, that he was comforted and unashamed. He did not need to know why I had done it, he did not need to know who I was, or remember what he had done for me. It wasn't a payment of a debt, not in the last count. It was an exchange of gifts.

It made me think, you know, that Jesus looked like somebody, I mean somebody real – I keep looking at people, people I know and just people in the street, and thinking maybe He looked like you, like that. At first I thought maybe I shouldn't think this, but now I think I should.

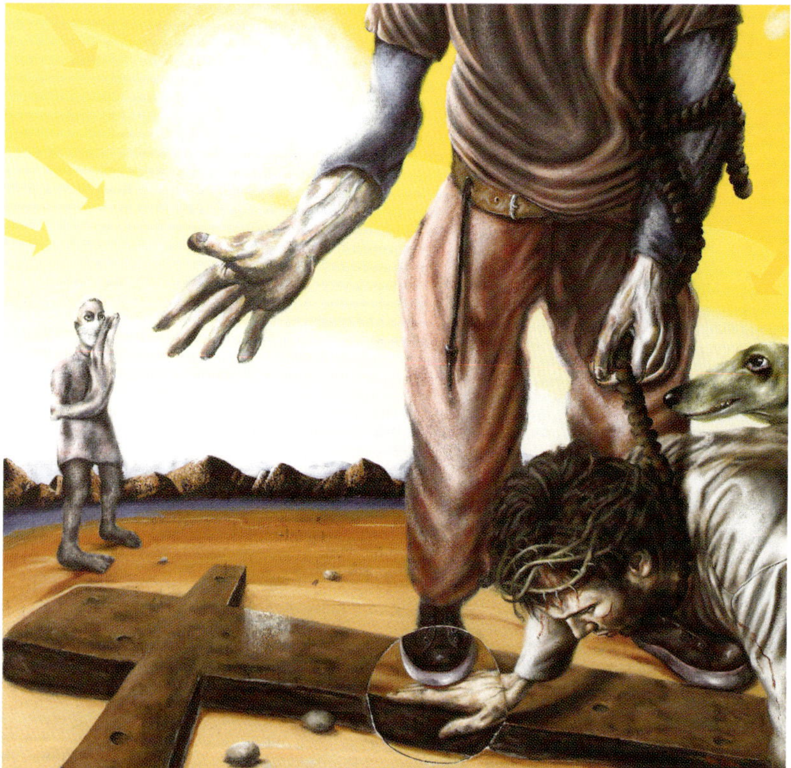

Station 7: Jesus falls for a second time

For a while, he is comforted.

It is easier now, with the blood wiped out of his eyes by those tender hands. He will never know her name: the woman he freed from pain and shame and who has come to repay him in kind with a precision as elegant and gracious as she is. She is a woman of dignity thanks to him as well as to herself, and he finds that consoling. Whatever this is all for, it is not for nothing, because she holds her chin high and looks squarely at a world she used to sneak about and grovel in. She can even afford gratitude; gratitude and courage – they are not nothing.

And he likes the presence of this man who, without even choosing to, forced by imperious circumstance, is carrying considerably more than his fair share of the weight. It is unbearably difficult to do a hard and generous thing when you have not chosen it. And when it is as physical and intimate as this is. And when you are as strong and fit and – he glances sideways – as good-looking as he is. It would have been easy, even pride-saving, to do as little and as meanly as possible, to punish the victim for the arbitrary power that has cast the task on you. He can feel the sadness of the man as well as the strength, but he is a man whose sadness makes him gentle not bitter, generous not cruel, so that he offers a consolation that is physical and solid.

He is lucky; he is blessed. "Abba, Father, let me do your will. Let me consent, like this man consents. Accept freely even though I can't choose."

"What's your name?" he says after a while. He knows the man's children's names; he knows the man's wife's name; he wants to know his name. It is good to call people by their names. He should have asked the woman her name, too. Names matter.

"Simon," he says.

Everything crashes down on him: a great wave of grief and pain. Simon. Simon Peter, son of Jonas. He had reached out to him, stretched out his love, across the courtyard last night; but Simon had seen only accusation. He could not reach him, could not tell him that it was all right: that to be Simon was to be a rich and wild mixture of courage and fear, insight and stupidity. But no, he had turned away; gone out into the dark beyond the firelight and, no doubt, wept like a child. Now he needs Simon here, not wrapped up somewhere else in a guilty sulk. He had guessed, he had warned him, but Simon never got it; he was always offering lots of noisy proclamations of everlasting love that were entirely, deeply sincere when he made them, but he had no capacity for the self-mockery and self-knowledge that sets a person free.

And it hurts. He knows Simon, he loves and understands Simon, but still it hurts. He had asked them to stay awake, to pray with him and for him and for themselves. And not just Simon: all of them.

"Watch and pray," he had urged them. "Stay awake. Watch and pray lest you enter into temptation." When he had wanted silence they would follow him, pester him, look to him like sheep without a shepherd so that he took compassion on them; but last night he had wanted them, yearned for them, needed them, even reproached them: "Just one little hour.. What's the matter with you all – can't you just give me a hour of your time?" But they had slipped away from him into sleep. And, blurred with sleep, they had not been ready; panicked by dreams and perhaps by guilt they had fled, melting into the night, leaving him alone to face the mob in the dark; priests and guards and . . . and Judas. He knows he does not know, does not understand about Judas; about what happened, what went wrong. Somewhere, somehow he failed this man, this lovely, clever, tough man, who had been his friend and companion for three years, and whose treacherous kiss was tender, almost apologetic. Judas had chosen clearly; Simon had jumped impulsively into cowardice. He had failed them; he had not set them free. But they had freely betrayed him, and it hurt.

As he so often does, he lets the pain pull him into the Scriptures, into the great shared experience of his people. This is something to thank his mother for, when all is said and done: they are there for him always, the great full-blooded songs she had sung for him throughout his childhood. They come to meet and absorb so many of his griefs and joys. So now he joins his pain to the Psalmist's:

> Even my bosom friend in whom I trusted,
> who ate my bread, has turned against me.

The love and the pain and the desolation overwhelm him; he flounders, catches his foot on a cobble, feels the nail of his big toe rip back from the quick with a purity of pain which is shocking, heart-stopping, and he falls, heavily. And the psalms fall with him, taunting him:

> A deadly thing has fastened upon him,
> He will not rise again from where he lies. . .
>
> You have caused my companions to shun me,
> You have made me a thing of horror to them
> And your waves have swept over me.

He cannot. He is beyond knowing what it is that he cannot do, but he knows he cannot do it.

Here comes Satan again, crouching over him; not jeering now, but comforting, gentle, offering relief, escape.

"You're His Son, His beloved – He said so. He transfigured you, with the radiance of heavens, whiter than any bleach.

"You are God.

"You shouldn't be here; you must defend the honour of your Father's house against these wicked people. They have no right to treat you like this."

It is the psalms again and he trusts them:

> He will give his angels charge over you;
> They will bear you up on their hands,
> Lest you strike your foot against a stone.

"Ask Him," says Satan, "ask Him."

"No."

"But he likes you to ask him; whatever you ask him he will do it. Ask him."

"No."

"You said so only last night; I heard you. 'Do you think I can't appeal to my Father and at once he will send me more than twelve legions of angels?'"

Groping on the ground, feeling the soldiers' contempt and the crowd's scorn, he knows he said something else; what had he said? What had he said in the wilderness the last time? His foot hurts too much; he cannot remember what he said, and Satan presses his advantage.

"Is this stubborn pride, that you won't ask? Or is it, perhaps, maybe, that you can't ask, because if you ask and He doesn't send those angels you'll know it was all self-delusion, that it is all for nothing? If you are the Son of God, he will give you anything you ask for. You daren't risk it. I think perhaps you don't ask because you don't quite believe. Go on, prove your faith; prove your trust. Ask."

"No."

"Why not?"

He struggles for it, "How then should the Scriptures be fulfilled, that it must be so?"

"Interpretation, interpretation. There are other ways to see it – you know that. The Christ will come with power, the Messiah with an angel army. Everyone knows it. It was when you said, 'It must be so' last night that your gang ran off. They knew it was a folly; they knew you'd lost your mind. You betrayed them, not the other way round. They needed you to take a stand, to live by what you said: 'Ask, and you will receive.' But no, not you. You've failed them."

The dark blur of pain begins to pass – instead, one of the soldiers starts to kick him, forcing him up. He can feel his second Simon getting angry. He might do something foolish and then what will happen to his boys? He has to get up; he has to move. But he kneels there exhausted, his head down between his arms like an animal.

"It's not too late," whispers Satan, "In fact, that might be what the prophecies meant, mightn't it? You were right last night; that was not the time or the place. The jubilee must be declared in Jerusalem, in Zion, in the Holy City. 'I was glad when they said to me, let us go up to the house of the Lord'. And now your feet are standing within the gates of Jerusalem. Standing! Stand up, ask and you will receive. Call down the Shekinah, the power of the living God from the Ark of the Covenant, and he will make your enemies your footstool. You were wiser than I. Last night was not the place or the time; this is the place and the time. Call down the angels, take up your power, cast out the invaders and reign. Go on. Do it. Ask."

"No. What would I say? 'Father, save me from this hour'? No. It was for this purpose that I have come to this hour."

"Oh, come on," says Satan, irritated. "Get real. The world's not like that. It's a half-baked scheme; your Father wouldn't have come up with anything so unlikely to work. He's not stupid, is he?"

Suddenly he feels something warm and wet, gentle almost; a healing touch on his foot. A stray dog has slunk up the street and is licking his wounded toe. There is a shudder in the crowd; the solid mass of bodies tries to draw back, away from him, and someone calls out "Jezebel". He is unclean.

God has rejected him.

Then an odd thing happens. The soldier who is yanking his chain and stamping on his fingers to make him get up, suddenly stops, squats down and pets the dog. "Good girl," he says, "good girl." He fondles her muzzle; reaches into the little bag at his waist, pulls out a bit of his own biscuit and gives it to her; then tugs gently and affectionately at her ears.

He looks round at the soldier and sees not a cruel conqueror but a boy, far from home and lonely for a puppy to play with.

"I don't know what it is with you," says the lad, grinning at him, slightly embarrassed, "Half the beautiful women in this city seem to want to clean you up."

Then he looks away, half ashamed. Shuffles a bit and offers his hand to help him up. "What is it about you lot?" he asks him and Simon, "Why don't you like dogs?" Simon shrugs, but he gets to his feet, swaying only slightly.

"Long story," he says, "but we do let them eat the scraps that fall off our tables." He grins, laughs at himself – another beautiful woman had taught him that, a Greek widow across the northern border; quick-tongued and eager, she had been, and with a knowledge of the scriptures as good as his own.

"Come on," he says to the boy, "Let's keep this show on the road. We've both got our jobs to do."

They get the cross up again, and this time Simon keeps his arm round him, warm and close like the dog.

He can laugh at Satan now. "I've remembered what I said to you the other time, out there in the wilderness: 'Don't tempt the Lord your

God'. He does not have to prove himself. One homesick kid and a stray bitch, that's all He needs. Legions of angels, indeed. Just clear off. Can't you see I'm busy?"

When I first saw some of these pictures I was upset because Jesus looks so angry, but when I saw this one I just thought, Well he would be angry, wouldn't he? It was a relief really. Now I can read him being angry in the Bible and I hadn't noticed that before.

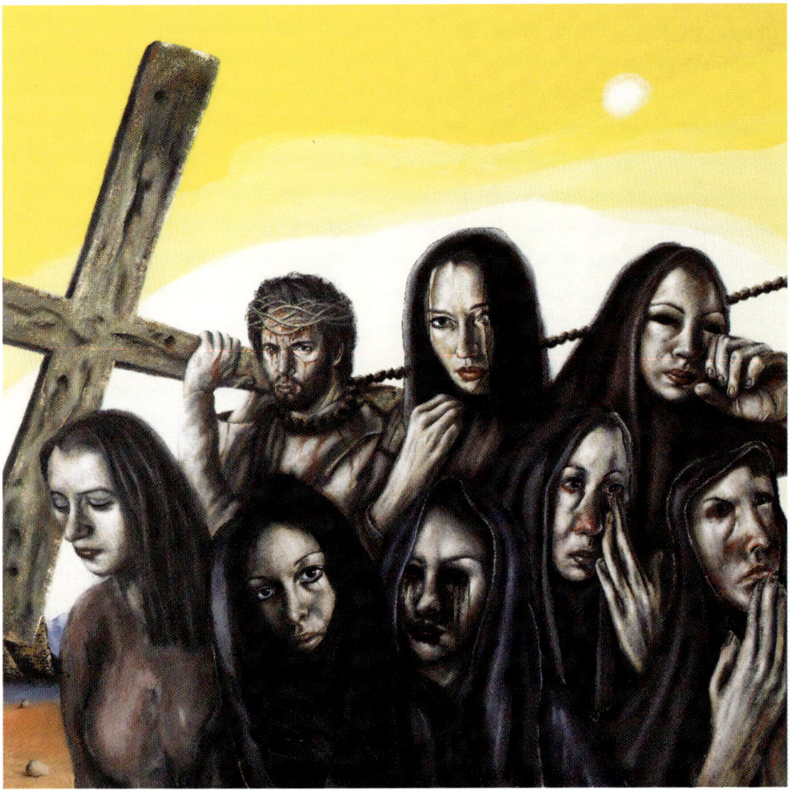

Station 8:
Jesus meets the Women of Jerusalem

We are the Daughters of Jerusalem. He called us the Daughters of Jerusalem.

We were nobodies, and now we are the Daughters of Jerusalem. A name gives you dignity and he gave us a name.

We probably do not deserve it; we certainly have not earned it. We were part of the madness. There had been a kind of madness in Jerusalem that week, and we were part of it.

We are the crowd who greeted him as King. "Hosanna," we shouted, "Hosanna to the Son of David," although he never behaved like a king. We ran about the streets, shouting and cheering, cutting down branches and tearing off headcloths to make a royal pathway for him; and he sat on his donkey and laughed, at us and with us, both at once. What did we think would happen next? Did we think we would see eye to eye the Lord restoring Zion? That wheat and wine would flow from the sky, and that the power of the living God would roll out of the temple and light up the whole city, like a fire that burns but does not consume? That justice and mercy would embrace, there on the cobbled streets; and that, with no further effort from any of us, the Romans would just pack up and go home? It was a kind of madness.

We are the crowd who flocked to the Temple to hear him. We pushed and jostled to get nearer to him, or to wherever gossip said he was. We laughed, and sang, and cheered when he smashed up the Temple market and threw over the moneychangers' kiosks. We revelled in his huge anger. We were running about the Great Courtyard, chanting his denunciations of the Temple staff, the scribes and Pharisees; jeering at them when they emerged, taunting them, teasing them, infuriating them. What did we think would happen next? Did we think that the Chief Priest would come out of his high house and announce the abolition of the taxes, throw open the treasury and renounce all his power? That all those fat cats, hand in hand with Herod, would turn and apologise to the poor and provide each woman with twin sons and an olive tree to sit under? That we would be admitted, all of a sudden, to the Holy of Holies, and be told the name of the Lord God Almighty and encouraged to rejoice in freedom? That they would become shepherds for us, and that, with no further effort from any of us, peace and prosperity would spring up like grass after the rains? It was a kind of madness.

We are the crowd who, only this morning, early and sullen, gathered at the Roman Governor's palace and bayed for his blood. "Crucify him," we howled, "Crucify him." Crushed together, swaying on a rhythm not of our own choosing, we chanted for the release of Barabbas, we swore loyalty to Caesar, and we shamed ourselves and our faith with our own shamelessness. We saw him scourged and beaten and bloody, and it made us angry, not with them or with ourselves, but with him. What did we think would happen next? Did we think that somehow his death would excuse our previous folly? That the Temple staff would forgive us for our disrespect if we did what they asked us now? That by getting himself arrested at all rather than calling down legions of angels for some cosmic spectacular – bread and circuses for the pious – he had somehow betrayed us? That God would reward us for our purity of heart, and that, with no further effort from any of us, we would be snatched up into the glory of the Lord and the freedom of the City of Zion? It was a kind of madness.

We are the crowd who bewailed and lamented him. Because, yes, there was madness and folly; but also there was a great sadness. He raised our hopes. He made us think that perhaps he was the one who would deliver Israel. He made us remember and believe again, that things do not have to be like this; that God is faithful, even when we are faithless; that there is a promise, and that that promise will be kept. There was something about him that called out to us: our brother, our son, our friend and, in betraying him, we betrayed ourselves. So we wailed and lamented – adding to the madness of the street and the anger of both the soldiers and the priests. We were howling and weeping and tearing our hair. What did we think would happen next? That he would be comforted by these paroxysms of hysteria? That he would forgive us? That, seeing and hearing our deep sadness, he would do something – take up his power and reign? We are women, we are good at grief; perhaps it was as much a guilt-letting as anything else – as though our mourning and keening would prove that it was not our fault, that we were on his side, and that we had not called for his death. It was a kind of madness, but a different kind of madness.

What we did not think would happen is that he would pause in his long, weary walk to his own death; that he would pause and talk to us.

"Daughters of Jerusalem," he said, "don't weep for me; weep for yourselves and for your children."

'Daughters of Jerusalem' he called us. It is from the women's song.

There are a number of women's songs in the scriptures: the song of Miriam, as the people danced to freedom across the Red Sea; the song of Hannah, as she nursed her longed-for son at her breast; the wild song that Deborah, Prophet and Judge in Israel, made for Jael the Kennite, to celebrate her victory over Sisera. But what we call the Women's Song is the Song of Songs, the love-song that God made for us. And the beloved says,

> I adjure you, Daughters of Jerusalem,
> By the gazelles or the hinds of the field,
> That you stir not up nor awaken love until it please.

He was weary; we could see he was so weary. He was in pain; we could see he was in such pain. He was betrayed by the people he loved, in the city he loved; we could see how deeply he was hurt. But he stopped in the street and talked to us. He gave us back the dignity that we had stripped ourselves of, in a kind of madness. He reminded us of our heritage; told us that we had responsibilities, and grief, and pain. He gave us a certainty that he knew and understood.

We knew he was teasing us when he called us the Daughters of Jerusalem, that he was aware how shallow our performed grief was, how near we had walked with madness. We were stirring up and awakening love for its own sake, not for his; for the emotional release and the tremulous excitement of passion. It was a kind of madness and, until we were healed of it, we would snatch at the next emotion, too, whatever that might be.

He said, "The time is coming when people will say, 'Blessed are the barren and the wombs that never bore and the breasts that never gave suck.'" We knew he was telling us that it is not enough to be a good wife and mother; that the blessings of childbirth are paid for in pain but earned in harsh loving, and in struggling for freedom for ourselves and for all children.

He said, "People will call on the mountains to fall on them and the hills to cover them." If we just stand around expressing our feelings on a hot, crowded street, there will be no hope, no future; and we will watch our children die.

He said, "For if you carry on like this when the wood is green what will happen when it's dry?" What will we do when it is not him but our own children? When there is real hunger, and real injustice, and real murder, and real desolation? We should not be wasting our time on these tears for him, but holding out for justice, and freedom, and peace.

He had no time – even while he was speaking, and before we could ask him anything, or thank him, or bless him, or even stop our foolish caterwauling, the Roman soldiers dragged him on up the street. The crowds pushed on after him, and he disappeared from view very quickly; we were left standing on the street corner, a bit bemused. There was no comfort in his words. If they were prophecies, the outlook seems grim. Had he reprimanded us, or encouraged us, or thanked us? We scarcely knew. But we did know that he had understood something about us that we were unable to understand about ourselves – and he had liked us for it.

Then something strange happened. We are not women who knew each other; not friends or family. We were just, so to speak, fragments of the crowd, who happened to have come together on a street corner and encouraged each other in a kind of madness. But, right there on that street corner, we turned to each other and began to talk about it. We were talking to each other, not as strangers but as friends.

At first some of the questions were odd and embarrassed – not the sort of things women usually speak about to strangers. For example, he had said, "Blessed are the barren." Was that a message to one of us in particular? We had to know: it felt important, and so we had to ask each other. Normally we know those things about the women we talk to, and we all tenderly talk around the difficult bits – but we were strangers, so we had to ask. And we stood there, asking and answering, and laughing and weeping again. The crowds had dispersed – gone on up the hill to the horror of Golgotha – but we did not go; we clung together, curious, excited, alarmed even. Soon, because it was preparation day, we had to go ourselves. We were busy with our lives, as women always are. But we needed to talk, we needed to understand and hold on to what we had been given; so we arranged to meet after the Festival, in the women's court of the Temple.

Because he had called us into friendship with each other, and had given us a name, we became the Daughters of Jerusalem.

The way we have described it is not quite how it was. It was all too strange, and hurried, and confusing. We do not all even agree about what exactly he said. We have gone back to the writings and argued about them, and gone over those few, brief moments. We know now we will not ever all agree; what we have here will have to do.

It is enough because, in talking about them, we grow together. In exploring, and arguing, and talking, we grow deeper in knowledge and clearer in thought. We know now that justice and mercy are hard to hold together; that real emotion hurts, and that pain can be better relieved by acts of love than by bewailing and lamenting. We know that sharp friendship keeps us safe from a kind of madness, and that fierce laugher gives women strength. We know that we can carry our responsibilities if we only pick them up in the first place. We know that "we" is a stronger word than "I", and that love is a stronger feeling than grief.

We know that he spoke to us with love.

We are the Daughters of Jerusalem. He called us the Daughters of Jerusalem.

We were nobodies, and now we are the Daughters of Jerusalem. A name gives you dignity and he gave us a name.

I like Station 8 because Jesus is speaking to the women; perhaps he will speak to me.

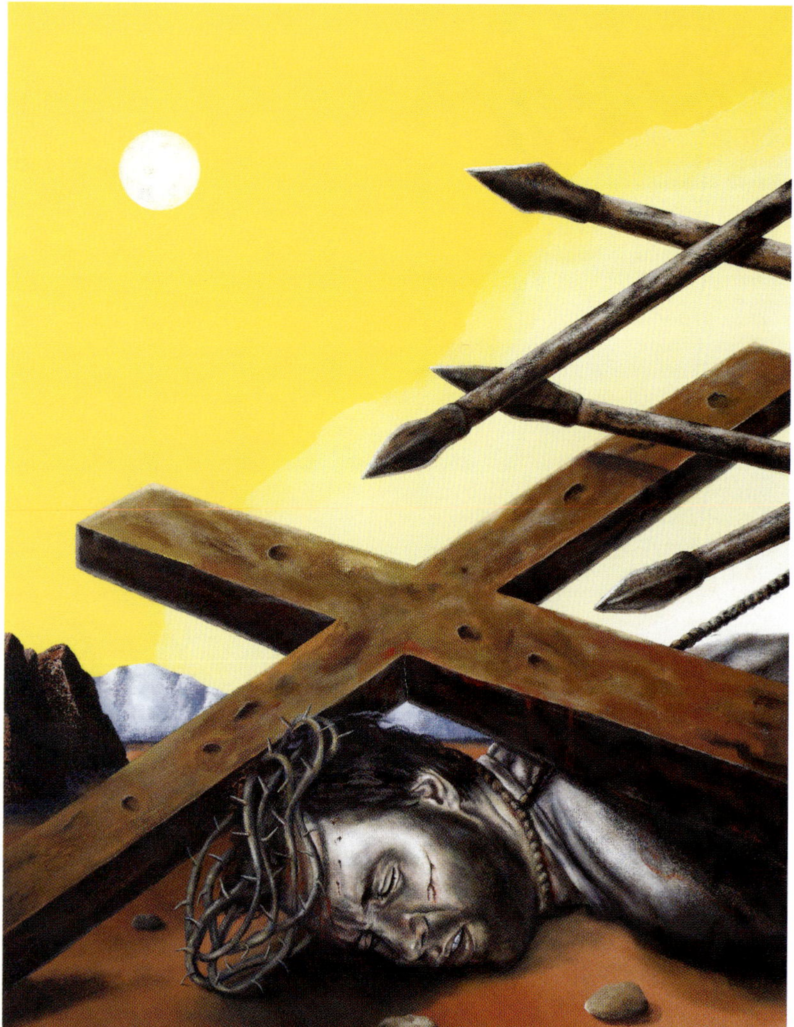

Station 9:
Jesus falls for the third time

After they go out through the city gates, he falls again. This time, he does not even know why. Perhaps he fainted. He has lost too much blood; been through too much pain; been awake too long. He hardly cares. His nose is bleeding; his mouth is clogged with its sweet, sticky taste. He cannot be bothered to open his eyes.

He is lying in the dust, pinned down by the cross itself. He knows he has pulled Simon over with him, that the two of them, without dignity and far beyond shame, are sprawled out on the ground, pinned down like insects under the thumb of God; and he does not care much.

Once they came out through the archway in the wall, under the Roman guardhouse and into the countryside, it ought to have been easier. The dense pack of people had space to spread out, loosen, unravel. There is less tension and more sunshine; he has been waiting for this moment, waiting to look into the distance, across the green valley to the hill country, up towards Bethany where he knows without question he is loved and honoured. The sun is bright on the hills and the great heights retreat solemnly into the distance in long ridges running north and south. On the nearest slopes he can pick out sheep grazing and olive groves, shifting grey-silver in a bright breeze; further away the hills look brown-tan and then, at the furthest possible range, dark blue shapes against the bright blue sky. But in fact, as they drag the cross through the ancient walls, he feel an enormous and heavy sadness; he will never come back to the Holy City again.

All his life, since before memory begins, he has been coming and going in this city, up and down the ancient streets, in and out of the

Temple. His parents had brought him here from Bethlehem when he was only a few days old, before they had left for Egypt and the years of exile. Here he was sacrificed for, and circumcised; here, his mother insists, he was prophesied over; here, each year, they had come on what was part holiday and part religious ritual; here he had run away and been soundly spanked for the anxiety he had caused them. He could still remember his sense of outrage, that it wasn't fair. He could still hear Joseph's calm, firm voice telling him that he was never again to do that to his mother. That if he wanted to stay and talk to the scribes and scholars he was very welcome, but he owed it – owed it – to his mother to tell her where he was and where he was going, for so long as she fed him and housed him and blessed him each evening.

"Be clear, young man," Joseph had said, "I am not punishing you for curiosity, for wanting adventures or for religious aspiration – I am punishing you for childish, thoughtless rudeness."

When Joseph laid one on you it stayed there; he had grown in wisdom and never again treated any adult with anything bordering on disrespect. "He just needs telling," Joseph had said to someone; and, even as he had tried to think that Joseph was unfair and didn't understand and wasn't his real father anyway, he could hear the deep pride and love in Joseph's voice.

And, year after steady year for over thirty years, he has come back again and again, just to be in the Temple; to taste the wider, brighter, sharper air of theological dispute and illumination, and to delight in their deep knowledge and his own growing understanding. Perhaps that is why they hate him now – because they had petted him as a child, and admired him when he was a young man, and wanted him on their side and he had not joined them, neither Pharisee nor Sadducee. He had taken his fierce love of the law and scripture out of Jerusalem into the wilderness, trekking after John or out there on his own; he had taken his honed knowledge up north to Galilee, or down into the Decapolis and Samaria – outside their territory, a clear declaration of independence.

How, he thinks vaguely now, does one balance respect and truth, when there is neither love nor honour to bind the two together, as there had been with his parents? Perhaps there was discourtesy in his great sonorous condemnations; perhaps it was not respectful to call them hypocrites and whitewashed sepulchres; but indeed they did tithe the dill and cumin and forget the common good. And in any case they were no longer his elders and betters – many of them now as young or younger than he was. Equal to equal, there could be no discourtesy.

Coming in through this gate only a week ago, the crowd had hailed him as their King. He had come home – to Abraham's promised citadel, to David's royal city, to the Temple of the Ark of the Covenant, to the altar of sacrifice and to the abiding city of God. He had come humbly, and been greeted excitedly. Knowing better, he had been caught up in their hopes, which were the hopes of Passover, of liberation and of triumph.

Here, less than twenty-four hours ago he realises with something of a shock, he ate the Seder Meal with his family, as he has done each year of his life. In that upper room he had used the old ritual to create a new one – a sign, a promise in itself. He is grateful for and delighted with that new meal; it holds body and history together and is centred in the city. In Jerusalem.

Now he is dragged out of his city as a prisoner and a criminal. He will never come back again. He sees the lovely, ancient stones pulled down and in ruins, the great muscular bulk of the Temple destroyed, and all the gardens and homes and shops and cobbled streets a haunt for jackals, broken and desolate. He came to his own people and they had not received him. He has been exiled from his own city. He has failed. He is too tired, in too much pain, too deeply betrayed, too sad to keep his balance.

A few paces beyond the gate he falls again.

He does not care. He lies there and waits to choke on his own blood. His mind loses its way and wanders off; the present folds itself up and leaves him only the past. He is a boy in Nazareth, and Joseph has released him early from his chores because it is so lovely an evening. From the hill above the village he can look down and see the distant shimmer of Gennesaret, silver in the long slope of the evening sun. There is a warm smell of sage and dry grass. Turning a corner under an outcrop of rock, he puts up a pair of gazelles, tan-coloured like the grass, and they take off, as deer will: a huge, leaping run that takes them over the brow and out of sight almost before he is conscious that he has seen them - the gazelles of the field, free and leaping in the last of the sunlight, and his heart leaps with them on the wide, sunny hillside; and it is so good to be alive, to be here, to be him. And later, later than he should have come home, his mother is laughing in the yard as he runs up the street towards her waiting arms; his mother is stroking his head as he lies on his sleeping roll, cool in a long blue evening; his mother is singing. She is not singing the psalms now, but her own song, his mother's song of joy and promise, that she had – she says – made up for him, when she knew she was pregnant and that he was coming to her and growing in her. She does not sing it often, not often enough, but she is singing now for him. She is singing, and stroking his hair and laughing. She is singing and she kisses him. She is singing. Singing.

Whatever his spirit may desire, his body desires only air; desires and demands it. He spits the blood out of his mouth, coughs up the blood in his throat, draws fresh air into his lungs and goes on breathing without either conscious choice or consent. He is not dead yet, not by any means; dying is not going to be that easy. The gazelles disappear, his mother's song ends, and he is lying on a different hillside in great pain, unwilling to move and vaguely aware that he cannot move because the weight of the cross has him pinned to the ground.

The serpent, gold and green and beautiful, uncoils herself sinuously from around the cross-joint of the cross. Her head is very close to his ear; she is whispering; her pink, forked tongue darts in and out and her black eyes are glittering. She says, "This is the tree of the knowledge of good and evil. If you eat of the fruit of this tree you will not die; your eyes will be open and you will be like God."

> This is the tree of the knowledge of good and evil.
> This is the tree of the knowledge of good and evil.
> This is the fruit that Eve offered Adam and they ate.

The serpent is smiling, but it makes no sense.

Satan is smiling too, now, a nasty, evil smile and he says, "So, your yoke is easy and your burden light, and you will give them rest? No wonder they ran away." He smirks a little as though this were funny. The beautiful serpent's eyes sparkle with spite.

They are lifting the cross off him now, encouraging him to stand up and finish his journey. Suddenly Satan kneels beside him, very close and very urgent. "Come now. Now is your last chance. Where is your God? He has forsaken you. If he existed in the first place. If you weren't mad. Curse God. Worship me. Look, you don't even have to humble yourself this time. You have already fallen down: you are grovelling. Worship me and I will make this death painless for you – quick and painless; as peaceful as falling asleep like a child, with your mother kissing you and singing."

Sleep, peaceful and without pain. He wants it so much. It is so easy.

But he has long habits of resistance, and a great deal of practice. He has that self-knowledge and irony that sets a man free. There is something odd about Satan – he is too desperate, too eager. He draws on a strength he did not know he had:

"Last time you offered me all the Kingdoms of the world and the glory of them; now you just offer me death."

Satan is shaken; this was not what he was expecting, but he is quick.

"I always offer the thing you want most. Then you were tempted; you were, you know – admit it. You were tempted by the power, and the glory, and the richness of the world. You don't want that now. What you want is for this to end. I will give you what you want."

The serpent, or perhaps it is his mother, is laughing. He is lonely and Satan is closer to him than anyone else will ever be. He wants it to end. He wants to go to sleep and never wake up. God is not here. Satan is here. There is no God. It is easy. He is tired. It is easy. Sleep, peace, and no more pain.

Then a thonged military sandal steps into the space where Satan's smiling face is; an anxious hand falls on his shoulder. "Please," says the dog-loving boy, who is too young to be a soldier, "Please. I'm going to be in so much trouble."

His vision clears: he can see the poor lad; he can see Simon, ready and willing, but needing to get back to his boys. This is his treasure; and where his treasure is, his heart is. With these lost and troubled men and women who have come with him up the long hill; his friends. He is the good shepherd, and he will lay down his life for his sheep.

He had made a mistake; there are not two commandments, only one, because they are the same. He still wants to sleep, he still wants peace and no pain, but he says,

"Be gone, Satan, for it is written, 'You shall worship the Lord your God and serve only him.'"

And Satan leaves him, the serpent disappears, and Simon of Cyrene and the pimply Roman legionary are the angels who minister to him; and he lurches to his feet, takes up his cross and staggers the last few yards to Calvary.

In the first eight Stations I love Chris's juxtaposition of imagined figures with real ones; arrows as cursors and as symbols of soldiery, creating a heightened form of reality. But from Station 9 onward that stops in a very arresting transition. Suddenly the spears are horribly realistic, sharply lethal: this is the time-stopping realization of what one human being can do to another.

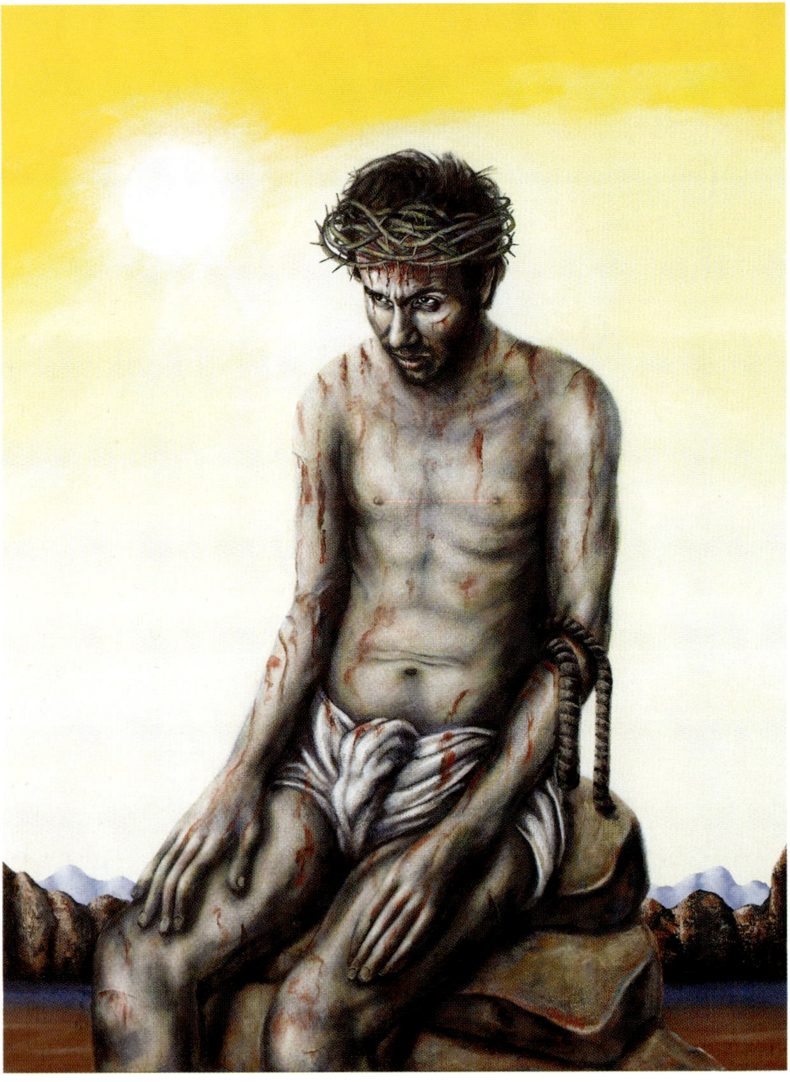

Station 10: Jesus is stripped of his clothing

Finally, they arrive.

They push the prisoners into a sort of holding pen while they get ready.

The place has been well chosen. The road running westwards from Jerusalem cuts below the hill and means there is a constant flow of traffic coming and going close by. There is nothing private or confidential about this Roman execution. They are clear-headed unsentimental rulers, serene in their power. Crucifixion is a public event, a statement of authority and a warning to others. The crowd is encouraged to watch; they are pushed back into a rough circle while the space is prepared and the crosses are erected. After that, and within reason, they will be free to mill around. But the centre of the circle tends to remain fairly empty, and even from the ground he can see over the city wall and into Jerusalem. Over the huddled roofs and narrow alleys the Temple Mount rises, and the fine new building with its own great walls, still not completely finished, faces him. From the cross itself he will be able, perhaps, to see down into the streets and marketplaces and see the bustle of people with better things on their minds than the execution of three minor criminals. It is preparation day, and every household will need to get itself organised and ready.

He had not realised there would be so much busyness. Just as they execute publicly, so the Romans also make their busyness very public. There is a lot of clicking of heels and jumping to attention. A lot of supervision, while the officers strut around inspecting the men and their work. Soldiers come and go. A delegation of Temple staff arrives. They want to make sure, he thinks wryly; they want to make sure that nothing goes wrong. He cannot at this moment imagine why they are still frightened of him. Or perhaps they are frightened of themselves. They are so well versed in the Law that it is not going to be perfectly straightforward for them to work out how to justify themselves for the bearing of false witness, and for working the crowd up to the point of acknowledging the authority of Caesar. He is even surprised they went about it this way – they would probably have done better to have given Judas a dagger and told him to slip it between the ribs as he came forward to kiss him. Though Judas would not have done that . . . he does not think that Judas could have brought himself to do that. If he were not so tired he would like to think more about what Judas has done and why. Poor Judas will get not get much joy out of the betrayal; he will not even be able completely to convince himself that it was really right and necessary. They will not treat him well; somewhere, the best of them will despise him rather than welcome him. He wonders vaguely how much they paid him for that kiss.

But a quiet assassination would have been cleverer of them in many ways. There was an odd wavering in their whole process. When he looks across Jerusalem at the Temple, shining in the morning sun, he can almost understand. If they really believed he had threatened the Temple, either directly or by stirring the people up into an ill-conceived revolt so that the Romans would destroy it, if they really believed that then he could sort of understand. It was so lovely; so courageous and brave. Jerusalem was their mother – all of them, him too. Love of the Temple and love of power had always been confused, always become entangled.

Then two soldiers come and strip him. He sits there while they take everything away. His clothes, his friends, his freedom. He recognises that he is still ashamed of his own nakedness, deeply ashamed. He is baffled by that shame. There is nothing left now but shame. His thoughts evaporate into emptiness. Even the pain retreats now he is sitting and does not have to move. He sits and awaits their will.

He is stripped to the bone. There is nothing left.

His mind is a desert. There is a hot yellow sun in a hot yellow sky. There are miles and miles of hot yellow sand, flat and featureless. There is no water, no shade, no birds, no horizon.

No words.

No memories.

No desires.

No fears.

They have taken everything away.

There is silence.

All his life he has loved and sought silence.

He knows that silence is a complex, lovely thing that comes with as many moods as the weather, blowing up from the East at dawn and in the evening. There are many places and many kinds of silence, and he thought he had explored them all.

There is the tender, intimate silence of the mother and the child after the night feed, when the baby is fed and at peace, without needs, and so learns to be alone and silent in the silent love of another.

There is the huge, fierce silence of the clifftop, the mountain height, the lightning bolt, the storms on the lake. The awed silence that transfigures the power and majesty of it all, that covers it in radiant light; a giddy, breathless silence in the face of the extravagant beauty and wonder of the world.

There is an attentive, listening silence, which opens the heart as well as the mind to the speaker and in that silence he has learned to hear. Mary of Bethany taught him that – more than any other person he knows she can listen; listen, and so hear. She can sit and listen, not uncritically or unquestioningly, but silently, collecting and holding meaning like a reservoir in the spring rains, holding water deep underground against a long dry season.

There is also another attentive silence, not dissimilar, perhaps the same even: a listening silence, that creates the space for someone else to speak into. A generous, patient silence, which combs out the tangled knots of human pain; which allows the oppressed to come to voice and declare their own freedom. He has always known that silence, and it is out of that silence that he has given people the power to heal and forgive themselves.

There is the silence of protest: the silent refusal to enter into the games and manoeuvres of the powerful. There comes a point where everyone else owns the words and uses them to their own ends, and leaves you none. There is the place of silence and of a dark judgement and freedom. They can whip you, they can punish you, they can mock and they can lie about you, but they cannot make you speak and your silence rears up as protest, and as power. There comes a time when you have to hunker down into the immoveable, heavy power of your own silence. This morning he had discovered that silence and its strength. It will be enough – just; and it will be everything.

There is the silence of companionship: of John's head on his shoulder, needing no words. The silence of long hours of walking with your friends, when the rhythm and the responsibility are shared and equal and there is nothing much to say, and no need to say it. This silence opens not into speech but into song; into music and laughter, and he likes to think that this is how heaven will be – food, and song, and laughter, at the end of a long trek home.

There is the ineffable silence in the presence of God: the formless, ecstatic silence of prayer, where the boundaries of the self dissolve and it is all given freely and joyfully. Love – somehow that silence is about love; loving, and being loved. It is given freely, and joyfully, and lovingly. The silence becomes the prayer as well as the way into the prayer. Words cannot encompass it and language fails. He thinks this is perhaps the silence of the mad too: the strange euphoria of possession; that is why he likes to be with them – he and they share something that most people try to evade. That silence is too perilous if it is not grounded in the certainty of love; it can carry a person away and they get lost in its farthest reaches where the words cannot go. Love grounds ecstasy, roots the ineffable, and keeps you safe.

There is the silence of the great cosmic forces, on which everything depends, although they are silent and invisible, as God is: light, and growth, and tides, and the turning of the days from morning to night, and the years from spring to winter. Air, earth, fire and water.

There is the silence of death: the doorway out beyond the words and into something else.

He is a free citizen of these silent places; he knows and loves them and seeks them out whenever he can, and wishes that that happened more often. Too frequently, some movement of compassion or urgency comes between him and the silence he craves.

But now the silence is terrible. There is nothing.

Perhaps God is silence. Perhaps there is no God.

"Abba, Father," he cries out silently, but there is no answer.

He is stripped to the bone. There is nothing left.

No words.

No memories.

No desires.

No fears.

No God.
They have taken everything away.
There is silence.

The silence of God is a very terrible thing.

I don't like them. They will change the atmosphere into something you would not want; they will make the church look gloomy and make you feel sad; but they are beautifully painted.

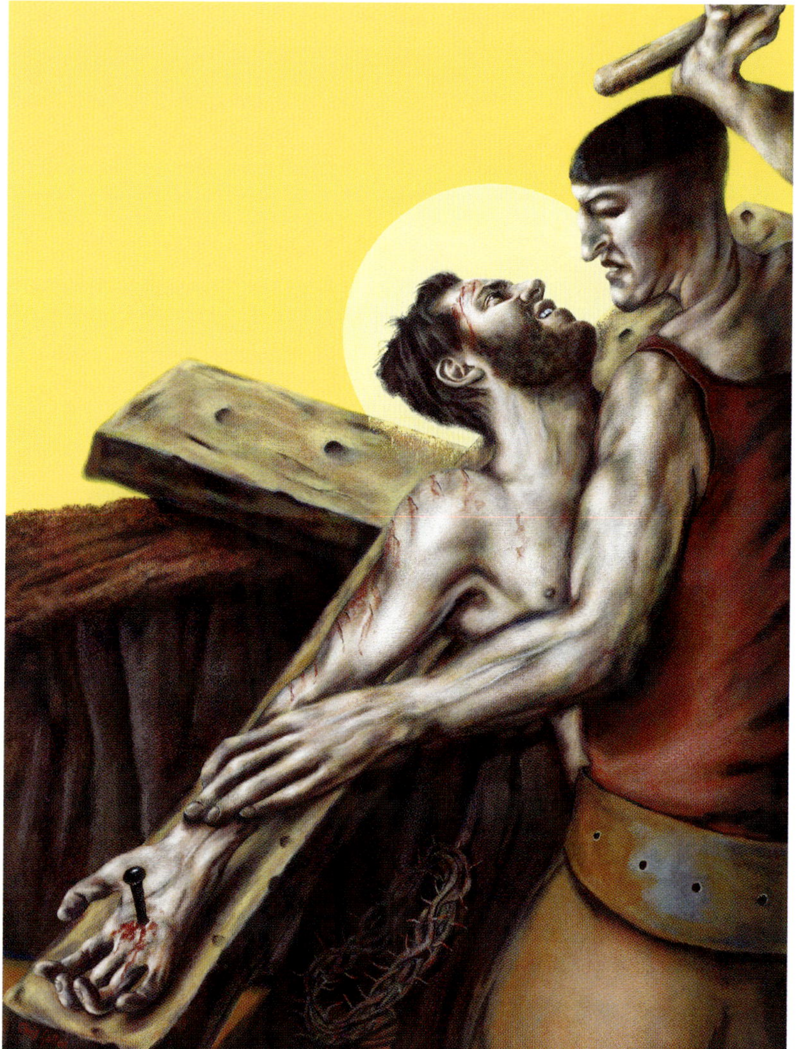

Station 11:
Jesus is nailed to the Cross

Today I am the hammer man.

As a matter of fact I quite often draw the job. It is meant to be random. The officer in charge is supposed to pick the whole crucifixion squad at random, and then just number off someone from that to be the actual hammer man, but not surprisingly it does not always work like that. For one thing – and especially when it's a bit sensitive like this one is, though I don't know why – you really do want the job done properly. I mean, we can do without the nails pulling out, or not getting their arms spread tight enough so that it goes on for three or four days; or hitting an artery so their blood is pumping everywhere and they're dead before you even get the cross up. For another thing, a lot of the guys really hate doing it and they can get all bolshy and difficult, and that doesn't help anyone. You might as well ask me and not have a fuss. And anyway, this time the Governor did not bring many of us up from HQ. At this time of year, with this religious festival going on, the city is crowded enough as it is without bringing a whole cohort up. Quarter-mastering is a bit of a nightmare at the best of times, because you can't call these people co-operative; and there's a running problem (or a not-running problem to be more precise) with the water supply. So it makes sense just to bring a smallish unit. The regiment down on the coast is on stand-by, of course; they could be up here in a couple of days if we needed them, so no one is complaining really, but it leaves us a bit thin on the ground, and there aren't that many other blokes around who can do it as well as I can.

Two of the convicts we're doing today have been waiting for a bit. I think the Governor was planning to hold them over until after this festival, but this morning we had a rush job. He's someone the locals brought in, which is a bit unusual; they don't often come to us for their religious things. Usually they like to do their own business, and let us get on with ours. But for some reason this was no knife-in-the-back-in-a-dark-alley situation; they wanted him strung up good and proper, in public and with the full works – Governor's Trial, regimental crucifixion, all Roman and correct. And they wanted to get him dispatched as quick as possible. So then someone thinks we might as well do the other two at the same time. It always looks a bit more impressive and, short-handed like we are, it's a lot easier too. Anyway, our officer comes into the mess shortly before we go on duty, lets us know what's going on and pulls out a detail and tells us the jobs. I've guessed before he gets to it that he'll say one more time, "You'll be the hammer man." And he does just that.

So, today I am the hammer man.

I don't mind, to be honest. I know why he always picks me: I'm good at it. I'm not one of those brainy types, so I rather like being good at something for once and having my officer know I'm good at it and appreciating that. And you don't have to be a brainy type to see why I'm good at it. I'm not cruel and I'm not scared.

Don't get me wrong. Crucifixion is cruel, no question. It's cruel, but I'm not cruel. I'm not scared of hurting them; I'm not scared of the cold-bloodedness of it (and you might well be surprised how many soldiers are – hot enough in battle all right, but then they go all nervy and squeamish about just taking some crook and banging him up); and I'm not scared of the gods. But I'm not cruel. I don't like to hurt them. I don't get any buzz off it (and likewise you might be surprised how many do. It makes everyone a bit queasy if someone really gets off on it). No, the way I see it is it's a job. Someone has to do it, and it might as well be done right.

So, when the others go off to march them to the hill, I report to stores and collect the hammer and nails. Nine of them, three for each convict.

The stores chap didn't have them ready. He faffed around for a bit and then counted the nails out, all slow and deliberate and fussy. They're not little pins, these nails; you've got to understand that. They have to carry a man's weight, and they have to go deep into the wood so he can't pull them out if he struggles; and the one for the feet has to be pretty long. I sometimes wonder why we don't do the feet separately, but you know the army – you do it the way you do it. So they are like big bolts, really, and nine of them weigh a fair bit; and you get them in a little sack to make it easier to carry them. But I take them all out again, right there in the stores and check they are all properly sharp. It's easier for everyone, including me, if they are good and sharp. Then I shove my thumb down on the wax tablet – though I can't read, so I have to trust that it says "one hammer and nine nails," and if I trust them you'd think they could trust me. But that's the army for you.

What with that, and crowds on the streets and so on, they all get there a good bit before I do, and when I arrive the prisoners have all been stripped already and are sitting in the pen, waiting. Now here's a tip. You might think I'd do the important one first and then carry on down, but I don't work like that. I took one look at him and I could see he was a quiet type. What you need to do is do the noisy ones first – the ones that are going to shout and yell and carry on – because once they are up they'll shut up, at least for a bit; somehow the pain does that to them, like someone hitting them in the guts. But, if they have to watch it happening, they tend to get more excited or something – a bit crazy – and nutters can be really strong. It's horrid to do it if they are screaming or blubbering, and it is even worse if they try and roll themselves up, pull in their arms and scrunch up their legs and try to fight you off. Normally it takes two of you to get them into position and hold them there, particularly with the first nail but, if you have a really strong bloke and he loses it, it can take five or six soldiers; and that upsets everyone and that's when things can go wrong.

So I start with one of the others, who looks a bit edgy to me, but it all goes pretty smoothly. Today we have new crosses, which also helps; obviously if you have to find a new hole in a cross that has already been used a number of times, it can prove a bit awkward. We have three new crosses on this job, so it's a lucky day from my point of view. Of course he screams and all that, and his body kind of jerks away, but they can't help that – they're not being difficult or anything; it's just something bodies do when you drive the nails in.

So I get the first two nailed, and then I go for the third guy. He's miles away, like he is looking out into some huge empty place and not seeing anything. I call him, but he doesn't seem to hear, so I just touch him on the shoulder; and then he comes back from wherever he's been inside his head and he stands up looking around. He is perfectly calm: I've never seen someone go to be nailed looking so calm. Some of them are very brave; you have to admire that, because where they are going is not going to be much fun, but his face was something beyond bravery: it was like he felt about the whole thing like I was feeling about the army earlier – you do it this way because you do it this way. It's a job; you just get on with it.

What you do is, you get them lying down centrally along the up-and-down bit of the cross, with their head dead in the middle. Then you stretch out their arms, trying to get the natural reach, not too tight and not too loose. And then, as quick as you can, you bang the nails in – no tapping or messing; it oughtn't to take more than about half a dozen whacks. I don't know why everyone imagines the nails go into the palms. Think about it: there's nothing there to hold a nail – you'd have it ripping out between their fingers within an hour or so and that would be really nasty. They'd tip forward and . . . well you can guess there's some skill in all this. You have to go in at a slight angle, right at the base of their hand; there's a whole lot of little bones in there, and there's a way through. If you get it right, the nail goes in easy, sort of slides between the bones; and then there's a solid pad of bones and muscles that will hold their weight for as long as it takes. As you go through, their fingers sort of clench up. The first time you do it, that can give you a bit of a shock – it looks like they're going to hit you, but it's just the way it happens; a reflex, they call it. Then with a bit of luck they pass out, and you can bend up their knees until you get their feet flat against the wood, cross them on top of each other and bang the third nail in between the long bones. When the cross is up they drop a bit; it puts a strain on their arms and after a while they find they can't breathe. So then they push up on their feet to take the strain, and obviously that hurts. In the end, it hurts so much that they don't do it, or they pass out; either way they die from, like, suffocation.

Well, with him, we get him lying down and stretched out quite easily. And I bang in the first nail. As I strike the first blow I say what always say, "May the gods go with you." His fist clenches up and he says something but I don't stop until I get the nail home, deep in the wood.

Then I look at him and say, "What did you say?"

He's white as bone, and he's biting into his bottom lip because of the pain, but he gasps out, "God. Not gods; there is only one God."

I go over to his other hand, and put the nail in place. And as I hit it I say, "May your God go with you." It seems polite somehow. I don't know why he made me want to be polite, but he did and there was no harm in it, so I just said it for him. And when I'm finished with that hand I look at him and he looks at me and he says, "Thank you."

Like I said, I do get to do more than my share of this job. But no one before has ever made me feel like it was a privilege to be his hammer man; that I have done something very important, and I have done it well.

"Good work," says my officer when we get back to the barracks.

"Thank you, sir," I say, saluting. We look at each other. I sort of want to ask him what the man was supposed to have done. I can't quite lose the feeling that, being that one's hammer man, I have done something important today. But my officer looks tired and I don't want to bother him, so I go down to the mess and get pissed as hell.

I find the whole series very challenging – such ugliness and pain. The yellow skies are very unsettling. I like them very much; so much more than the usual sanitized Stations. It is very rewarding interacting with them.

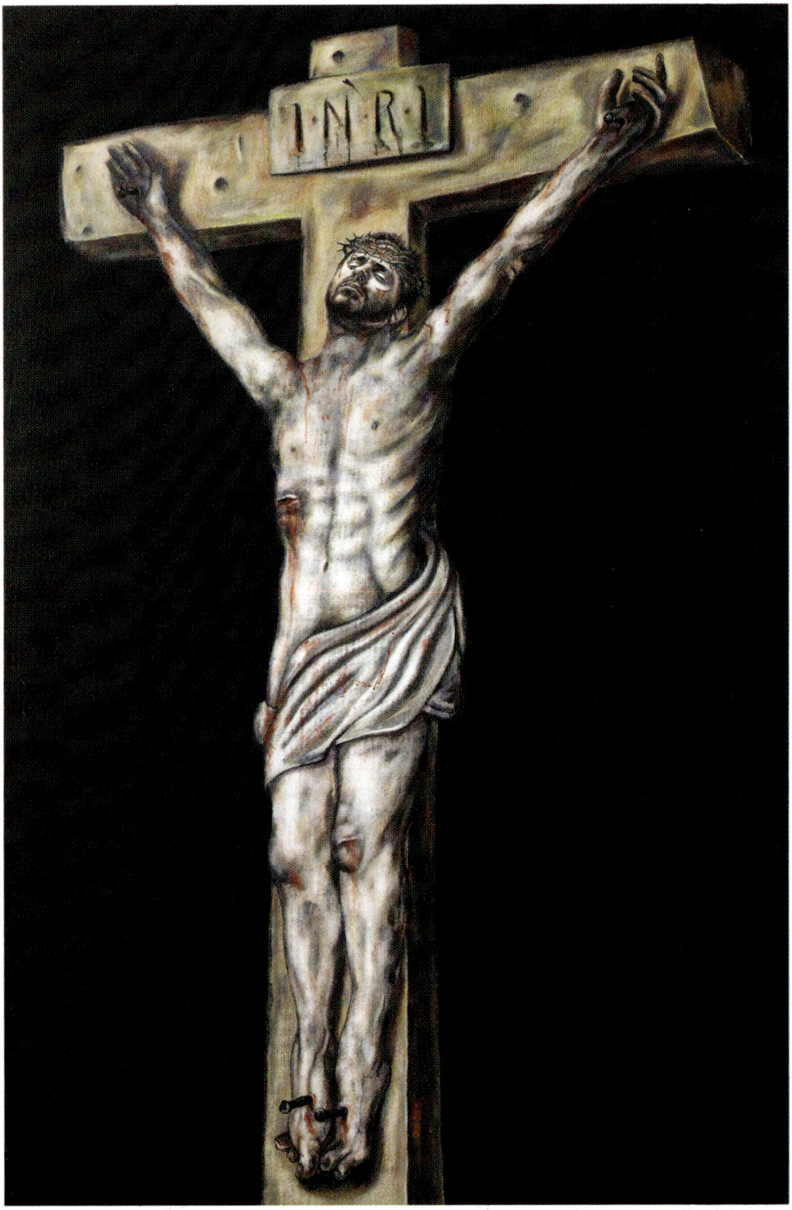
I·N·R·I

Station 12: Jesus dies on the Cross

Finally, in the late afternoon, he died.

It took a long, long time. I did not know it would take so long. I did not know how much the human body was capable of enduring. I didn't have the first idea.

If I had known how long it was going to take, I would never have told him that I would stand there until he died. It was the last thing I said to him. It seems now like an obvious thing to say, and I am glad I said it; and even gladder that, having said it, I did it. But I would not have said it if I had known.

When they took him away last night, we did not know what would happen. It was dark; there was a fair amount of muddle; we were tired and shocked; we were frightened. They took him away, and we were left with the muddle and confusion, and blaming each other, and getting angry with him. Through the night, all we had was rumour. We were all running round the city, avoiding each other because we were frightened and angry; needing each other because he was not there and, above all, wanting to know what was happening. Nobody really knew anything at all, and we all tried to fill the aching gap with speculation, and gossip, and guesswork; and we were all more and more confused and angry.

And in the morning there were crowds baying for his blood. It was horrible. It was so horrible. It was a lynch-mob getting itself wound up for a stoning – but it was too many people for a lynching. Everyone lost a sense of themselves, like animals in a storm, and there was this strange noise, between a howl and an enormous mutter. I can't explain. I could not bear it. I went back to the house, but there was no one there; just that awful, crazed chant, "Crucify him, crucify him," rolling about the streets, bouncing off the walls, with no sense of what direction it was coming from or who was shouting it.

And I knew, when I heard that crowd, that they were going to kill him. I wanted someone to hold me, someone for me to hold on to; but there was only him, and he needed holding. And . . . in the end I needed him just that little bit more than I needed to be frightened or angry or confused. I needed him, so in the end I went up the hill. I didn't really go for him, to help him; I went because I needed to go.

Then, when I got up to the place, there was something else. From that hill there is a view over the whole of the city, and you can see the Temple, and a wide spread of the countryside, right across to the mountains. He had a thing about Jerusalem and when I saw the view I thought that he had chosen this place and that he was going to do something. I wasn't sure what, but something spectacular – everything was going to be all right.

More than all right.

I was divided: one part of me was desperate, and howling inside because he was going to die, and the other part of me was thinking, "He called Lazarus out of the grave. He is the Messiah. Now, any moment now, he will do it." Whatever IT was. So that part of me was excited. I felt a sort of contempt for my own fear and for those of us who had not come to watch it, to be there. I felt sorry for them.

I've never been to a crucifixion before. I thought somehow it would be grander; I think maybe I expected more: more soldiers and horses and trumpets, and some grand Roman carrying on; something with a bit of pomp and dignity. But it wasn't like that; it was sort of sordid really – no ceremonial or ritual. There was a lot of milling around, and hanging about, and coming and going. Every now and then the soldiers would sort of push the crowd back and shout at us, but not with much conviction. I didn't know what was going on, so I just waited.

Then he arrived, but I could not really see him. They put him in a pen like an animal. I pushed my way forward, to get closer to him. But when I saw him . . . he is my friend, but he is also like God to me. I believed he was the one who would set Israel free; that he would restore the Kingdom, and we would be dancing in the streets, and there would be joy, and abundance, and promise. But when I saw him in the pen, I knew that he was not going to Do Something – or anything; that this was the end, and he was going to die. I have never seen a person look so alone, and defeated. He was pretty bashed up and bleeding – they had not treated him gently – but it wasn't that; they had stripped him naked, but it wasn't that either. It was his face: he was desolate.

It broke my heart.

All I wanted then, for one pure moment, was to comfort him. I called out to him that I was there, and I would not go away. I would stand with him to the end. I don't even know if he heard me. He didn't look up. But I had said it.

I did not turn away, even when they banged the nails in, although it made me sick. I just leaned forward and was sick on the grass and wiped my face with a corner of my shawl and looked at him. I was determined that I would not take my eyes off him.

That was before I knew how long it takes.

It was hot in the sun, burning hot, and I had promised him to stay standing. I did not even want to move, because he could not move. The sun was as hot on him as it was on me, and he was naked. I had told him, even if he had not heard me, that I would stand with him. So to move, even to sit down, would be a betrayal, and he had been betrayed enough. At the beginning I was quite emotional; I was angry, with him, and with myself, and with everyone who was not here; and proud of myself, and proud of him, and terribly, terribly sad. But soon I was too weary and too drained to bother with any more emotions. There was nothing I could do for him except stand and watch, so I stood and watched.

Shortly after noon, I had another idea: I took off my veil, and pulled out the long pins, and let my hair tumble down my back. He loved my hair; he said it was beautiful; he hated me to wear a veil. When we were in the hills I'd take it off, even though some of the others were shocked. Now, here, in this very public place, letting my hair down announced to everyone who wanted to notice that I was a whore – respectable women don't let their hair down, and mine is pretty blatant. I could feel a frisson of shock in the crowd, and I heard a couple of lewd comments, too; but I did not care. I didn't think it through then, but I have now. Partly it was because he was being humiliated and I wanted to be as close to him as possible, but it wasn't mainly that. It was more because, if he could still see, still register what was happening, still care, it would remind him of those days in the north – of sweet breezes in the standing corn, of the glory of the lilies of the field, and of those long evening of wine, and singing, and laughter.

It was a joke between us, my hair. Once I dried his feet with it, for the simple delight of teasing him, and shocking those dreary creeps he was eating with. I got myself all tarted up, rather literally - hitching my boobs up in a cheap but glittery gown, and all the hair fluffed out and curling wantonly. Then I sashayed into the middle of the dinner party. He was, as usual, talking, talking, leaning on the table and talking, but when he saw me he grinned hugely, both at me and at the undercurrent of nervous shock that ran round the room, because inevitably I knew some of those worthy and sanctimonious citizens pretty well from my working life. Some of them weren't just shocked that he should let a prostitute appear in their company, but also terrified of what she might do or say. We understood their fear, and we laughed at them; and they would never forgive him.

And that, I realised, was why he was here. I knew that it was that joke - not just my joke, but my own joke among other things – that ended him up here. We pushed our luck too far in the hill towns of the north, just as we pushed it too far in the market and the temple courtyard this last week. We touched too many people's fear and pride and self-loathing with our joyful freedom. I accepted that I, as much as any rabbi or Temple lawyer, as much as the Roman tyrant, as much as the soldiers who were sitting around, bored and playing dice while he died – I as much as any of them had brought him here. And at the same time I knew absolutely that he would still have grinned hugely, he would still have laughed with me against their hypocrisy, he would still have laughed and loved, even if he had already heard the sound of the nails hammering through the bones in his wrists.

Then it stopped mattering whether he could still see or hear or notice. I didn't mind what anyone thought or said, I let my hair down just on the off-chance that he might sense it and be comforted. It wasn't much, set against what he had given me. I decided this afternoon in the long, hot dying that I will never put my hair up again, never cover it over and pretend to be respectable – I will take the freedom he has given me and live it for as long as I can.

Not that these fancy thoughts did much for me at the time. I just stood there and wondered why I had made such a stupid, half-baked promise and prayed that, now I had kept it up this long, I wouldn't pass out and fail him. Various other people came and went: his mother, some of the other women – mostly women, though John was there for a while, I think. Someone offered me a drink of water, but I couldn't accept because he had none.

At the beginning he spoke a little, although he was in great pain and very tired, and there was nothing much to say. He muttered a bit now and again. I think he was reciting from the psalms, but only because he always did that. I couldn't really hear him. Later, he fell silent. You could see him struggling for breath. It was terrible. He'd slump down, hanging from his hands, but then he couldn't breathe out properly so he'd push up on his feet, and you could see the pain – his beautiful feet, which I had dried with my hair.

I think the sun went dark. Or perhaps it was just that my whole world went dark. At one point I found myself silently urging him to get on with it, to die, to let go, just not to bother about getting another lungful of air. We'll cope, I told him. We'll look at each other. I probably meant we'd look after each other, but "look at" was what he always did, so it may have been right. I just wanted this horror over and done with, partly for his sake and partly for mine, because the whole thing was unbearable. And there was nothing to do except bear it.

I don't know if it made any difference, my being there. I suspect really that it was the same as in the morning: I didn't go up the hill for his sake, but for mine, because I needed to. I didn't stand there all day to comfort him, but to comfort me because I needed him.

But, finally, in the late afternoon, he died.

It's sad but simply beautiful.

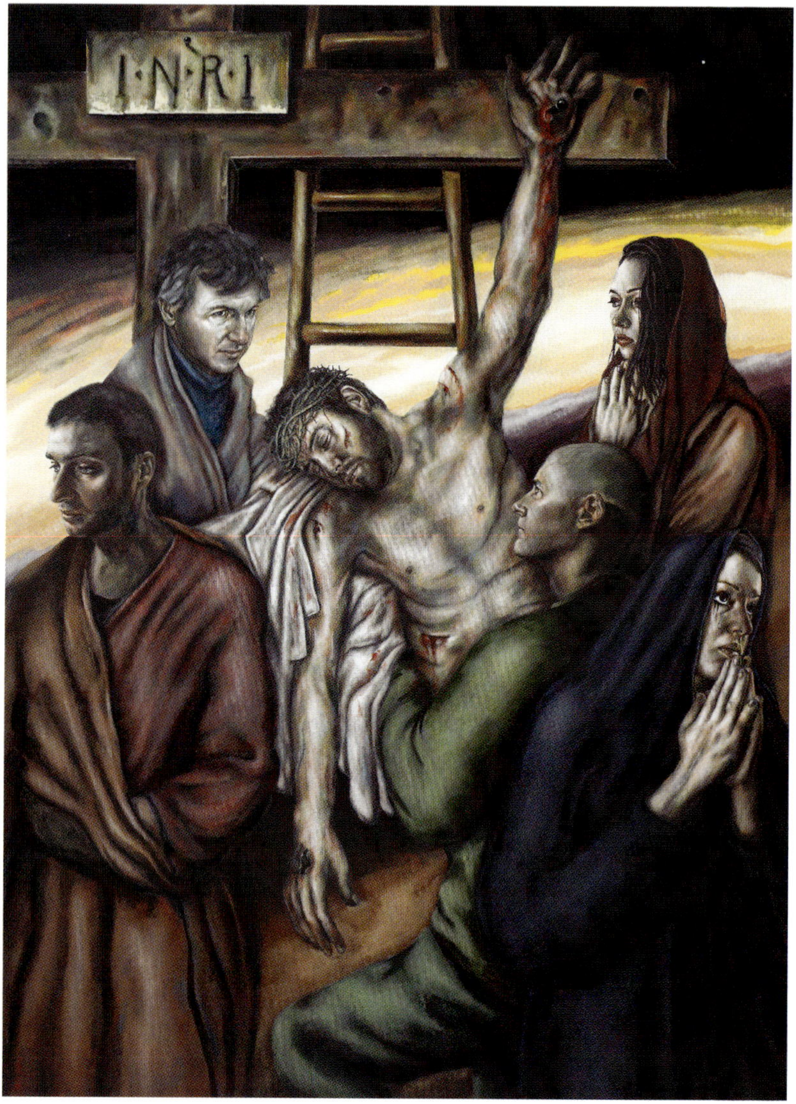
I·N·R·I

Station 13:
Jesus is taken down from the Cross

And, just when you think you cannot take any more, you find that you have to.

Sometime in the late afternoon, he died.

I thought I was watching. I was watching; but I cannot say I saw him die. He had gone past speech, past the hideous struggle for breath, past anything, really. Perhaps he died the moment he dropped his head forward, but I think he was still alive then. I think he chose his time; I have to think that – that he chose, finally but freely, to stop struggling for each breath, and let his head fall forward, and die. But I did not notice the exact, precise moment. I wish I had. I wish I had stayed with him to that very edge; I wish it now because I slept in the garden, even though he asked me to stay awake with him.

I knew he was dead, because Mary moved. She had stood there all day, as near to him as she could get. She just stood there and watched him. There was something terrible about her still watching, and also something beautiful about it. Now though, quite abruptly, she turned, took a couple of steps away and then sank down to the ground. It was quite strange because she did not fall over, or faint, or throw herself down, or any of those things. She went down slowly onto her hands and knees, like a very old woman, and then sort of curled up sideways and lay on the ground, all huddled up. I knew then that he was dead, though when I turned to look at him I could not tell. I trusted her though; I had to. She would not have moved unless he were dead, however she knew that.

I would have gone to her, despite all the trouble between us, but I had been given a duty. So I looked for his mother and put my arms round her, a little hesitantly because I could not tell what she would really want. But she leaned against me, and I held her.

Then nothing much happened for a while. I stood there with my arms round his mother, but she did not weep; she just leaned against me and was almost completely still. One of the other women came and sat down beside Mary and held her hand, but she did not move. I realised she was too tired to move. We were all too tired, perhaps too tired even to feel; so we just stood around and nothing happened for a bit.

Then one of the soldiers came up and inspected him and shook his leg. "He's dead," he said, sounding a bit surprised. No one said anything. Then, almost casually, he stabbed him in the stomach with the short spear they all carry. It was shocking – the suddenness and the force of it. He pulled his spear back out and the wound bled, with a strange mixture of blood and water. I just stared at it, trying to make some sense out of what was happening, but one of the women screamed at the soldier, "What did you do that for?" And he said, "Sorry missus; we have to do that. Someone's got permission to take the body, and we have to make sure he's properly dead before we release it." We looked at each other, baffled I think.

Then they arrived.

So, all right, they meant well, but I, I hate them. I hate all those posh types who make you feel, in a kindly sort of way, that you are in fact provincial scum; the kind that makes you want to go up to them and say, "My father owns his own boat," whereas most of the time you never think of it and don't care either. Mary had stood there all day, all that long, hot, horrible afternoon and now they arrive and just ignore her.

They've brought the right things - a ladder, a nail-claw, a shroud – and I know I ought to be grateful, but. . .

Nicodemus says, in that high, grating voice those educated Temple types all have, "Joseph went to see The Governor himself; he went and asked if we could take the body and bury it. And Pilate said we could."

I can tell from the way he says "himself" that I am meant to be very grateful, and also full of admiration for his courage and his thoughtfulness. There is nothing in that voice which indicates that he even realises that if I – if any of us – had gone to the Governor's house and asked to talk to him about releasing the body, we'd have been thrown out on our ears and probably whipped for lack of respect into the bargain. I'm not saying it wasn't good of him to bother; I'm saying they shouldn't be so pleased with themselves.

These two are what we called "fly-by-nights". They liked Jesus; they liked what he said and they really did want to talk to him. But they did not want to be associated with him, and certainly not with the rest of us. So they would turn up, late in the evening when it was dark, wearing voluminous cloaks and hoods. They'd slink up to wherever we were, looking both smug and nervous. Then they'd expect him to talk to them. They did not want just to sit with the rest of us and see what happened. They didn't want to sing, and laugh, and tell stories, and have a drink. They would never give anything personal away; never share stories, or laugh at themselves, or tell you about their childhoods, or any of that sort of normal chat. They would slip off into the dark when they were done and were always embarrassed if you saw them in the street in the daytime.

They wanted to have proper, educated conversations, and ask complicated theological questions. All the time, we would feel they were looking for him to get something wrong. They weren't like the hard-core priestly thugs who wanted him to say something wrong so that they could have him arrested, or at least wind the crowd up. No, it was different from that; in the end, we came to think that they wanted him to say something wrong so that they would be free not to commit themselves. They knew what he was, or something of what he was anyway; but they wanted any excuse not to have to deal with that. They were like little, scared boys, showing off, pleased with themselves, but not wanting to risk getting caught.

Nicodemus knew. He said so – "You are from God," he said to Jesus, "you do all the right things." But they say that, when the Council sent those investigators to find out what we were up to and they went back without arresting him, there was a great deal of discussion about us. And Nicodemus – well, he was not going to say there that Jesus was "from God", was he? Not in front of all those grand, learned thinkers and temple rulers, and collective hypocrites. They might have laughed at him; they might have been cross with him. So he doesn't say anything, and then he clears his own guilt by raising some point of Law about how they can't condemn us without some proper hearing. They all sneer at Galileans, and Nicodemus comes over at night to tell us all about it.

They just do not get it. I remember the morning Andrew came by the boats. Simon was getting kitted out alone, because his brother had gone off somewhere; and we were helping him out a bit, because there were the three of us – James and me and my father.

Andrew appeared; he stood above, on the edge of the grass, maybe ten or more paces away, not wanting to waste any time, and he called out, "We have found the Christ."

We all looked at each other, and then my father sighed and said, "Well, off you all go then," and we did.

So now, three years later, I think about that; about my father, alone in the boat but whistling as we walk off up the hill. And I just cannot bear to have these two here. I want to tell them to piss off; that they weren't here when he needed them, and we don't want their hoity-toity, patronising presence now. We don't need them admiring their own fine courage and expecting us to be grateful, on top of everything else. We can manage.

Except we can't. I know we can't. Simon's down the bottom of the town, weeping in a darkened room – not very helpful. I don't know where anyone else is. Mary's out of it for the moment. I've got to look after his mother. And I know for a fact that the Romans won't let us take his body away - even if we had anywhere to take him, which of course we haven't. I am too tired to think it through cleverly.

So I say, a bit aggressively probably, "Where are we taking him?"

Joseph doesn't hear the aggression. He says, "I own a garden, just below the hill."

He would, wouldn't he? A nice little garden, only a Sabbath stroll from the city walls. I mean. He goes on, "I excavated a tomb in it, just a couple of months ago. We're going to put him there."

He is up the ladder now, tugging the hands away, dragging the nails out. It is horrible; I try to watch, but it is horrible. I don't know what to do. Then I feel his mother move against me, and I look down and she gives me this wink. She's exhausted, heart-broken, emptied out, but she gives me a huge great wink. She knows exactly what I'm thinking, and she agrees with me; and she has decided that it's best to go along with them. So I shut up.

She draws away from me and sits down on the ground, and says with so much dignity, "Bring him to me, please."

I can't watch while they get the nail out of his feet. It makes me feel sick and I turn away. When I turn back, they are carrying him over to her; and they lay him in her arms, with his head in the crook of her elbow, and she puts her other hand on his cheek and just strokes his face very gently. I see the tears well in Nicodemus' eyes and I sort of try to forgive him because, really, he cannot help being the rich, posh git that he is.

After a little bit his mother calls over to Mary; she asks her to come and help wash him. A long, bleak day; all the utter, hideous vileness of crucifixion; her only son – and still she will ask for help, because Mary wants to help and will be comforted by helping. That's the difference, really, between Nicodemus and her. She doesn't even think, "Mary's an ex-hooker." She thinks, "Mary will want to help, will want to touch him, be near him." She will not own her own son, not even in his death.

Now Mary crawls over to her and she is crying, great wet tears; and her hair flows over his battered body and his mother holds his head in her arms. They wash him. The two of them wash him together, so calmly and sweetly. It is very sad, and very beautiful, and I want to watch them forever.

Too soon, though, Joseph goes up and says that they must hurry up now. Mary looks at him with a big question on her face, because there is nothing for her to hurry for any more. Joseph says that they need to get him buried before sunset or they'll all be unclean and won't be able to participate in the rituals tomorrow; and I can see both women smile, because clean and unclean and tomorrow and all those other words don't mean anything now.

But Joseph and Nicodemus are quite urgent, impatient, pressing them. They unroll the shroud on the ground just beside the body, and look as though they might snatch him out of her arms. I can see she is annoyed, and I'm a bit surprised that they can't, or don't seem to notice.

"John," she says, "Can you come and help us?"

"Yes, mother," I say. It is the first time I have called her that and I can feel my own mother approving.

So, as gently as I can, I lift him out of her arms; his head lies on my chest, as mine lay on his at supper last night. Even then they can't resist doing things. Nicodemus lifts his legs for me, but to be honest it is genuinely helpful now. We lay him on the shroud. The two of them wrap him quickly, and then Joseph, Nicodemus and I carry him to his grave in the garden.

I want it to be peaceful and it isn't. You can see how difficult and complicated it must have been. All those people flocking round and being busy makes it much more like an ordinary sort of death.

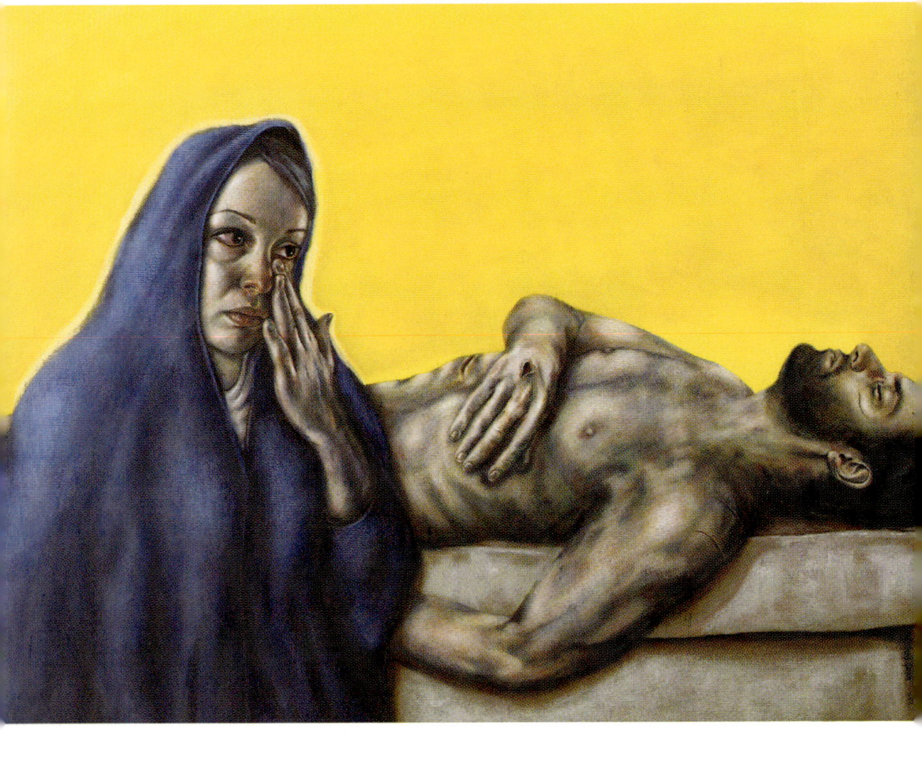

Station 14: Jesus is laid in his grave

They carry him to a nearby garden where Joseph of Arimathea owns a fresh grave; a cave in the hillside, looking out over Jerusalem.

They are in a hurry now. They need to have him buried before the sun sets, or they will not be in a state of Preparation and so unable to celebrate the next day's feast. This bothers them to various different degrees, but Joseph has somehow taken charge and it bothers him a great deal. They all go along with him because they are all way beyond arguing or making any alternative plan.

Mary of Magdala washes him again, briskly and efficiently, her long hair falling forward to cover the worst of his wounds so his mother does not have to look at them. For now, they wrap him hastily in a shroud and cover his hands, feet and face with some cloths. His mother produces from somewhere an ornate, beautiful, ebony-and-silver pot of myrrh. Nicodemus and Joseph catch each other's glances of surprise. She does not explain. Around that, they pile up the rest of the almost ridiculous quantity of spices and preservatives they seem to have collected.

The women will come back after the Sabbath festival and do the job properly. For now, this will have to do. They have run out of time, and ideas, and energy.

Just as they are finishing these sketchy arrangements, a detachment of Pilate's guards arrives, with orders to seal the tomb. They are in a hurry too, ordering the women out of the tomb with an apparently callous haste. As she turns away, his mother begins to wail. She has been silent all day but now she starts keening, an almost crazed howling. It is nearly unbearable. Partly to make her stop, partly to make it easier for her, they all hurry out of the cave and let the guards do what they have to do. They stand, a small, depressed, baffled group, a little way away, watching while the soldiers push a single great stone over the grave entrance and seal it with wax and rope. Then their officer calls them to order. They form up neatly and march off at the double.

After that, there is nothing to do. So they do nothing for a while. Eventually John puts his arm round Mary and leads her away. The rest of them follow. The sun slips behind the western skyline.

He is dead.

He is dead, and the world goes on turning. Why has it not fallen in on itself? What sustains it?

They do not know. They are past caring.

He is dead.

Painting your own son dead – it was the most difficult thing I had to do.

Chris Gollon

AFTERWORD

Afterword
by The Reverend Alan Green, Team Rector of St John on Bethnal Green

At the heart of the Christian tradition of the Stations of the Cross is the sense of pilgrimage — a journey to a sacred place as an act of religious devotion. Not surprisingly, Jerusalem has been a major focus for Christian pilgrims to engage with the life of Jesus and, as a pilgrimage within a pilgrimage, to follow in Jesus' steps, from his appearance before the Roman authorities through his last journey to the place of his execution and burial. Meditating upon those events and their significance in the very place they happened can have a huge effect on individuals, bringing their own life stories, their faith, intellect and emotions into contact with one another in a life- changing way. Marking those Stations, those points on Jesus' way of the cross, within our churches has been a means of participating in that pilgrimage; sharing a little of that experience whilst remaining at home. Consequently, the major use of the Stations in church has been in an act of peregrination: walking around the building, stopping at each marked point to reflect or pray upon that particular theme, and allowing the points of contact between what happened to Jesus, what happens in our world and what happens to us to mingle together.

The walking is important. There is certainly a place for stillness in churches, but such stillness can easily be replaced by a cheap holiness that is characterised by a sort of shuffling embarrassment, not allowing our spirits to soar, but rather to cower in apprehension. Out of that apprehension we try to departmentalise, to create simple categories that make the chosen feel safe. The obvious example of this is the effect in cathedrals of making simple distinctions between those who have come to have a look round and those who want to say a prayer; that is, between those who have to pay and those who do not. The purpose of those buildings has always been to get people to look at the wonder of their artistry — in architecture, in stained glass, in painting — and to add a religious dimension through the experience. If the art is any good, and if the religious authorities have any sense of spiritual development, the beholders should be free to interpret and respond to those impulses as they will, and not have a single meaning imposed upon them. Recognising that cathedrals must raise their income, I guess I would be happier for people to pass through the tills at the exit rather than the entrance; if they were unable to remember anything that they saw that excited or challenged them, moved them to prayer or to annoyance, then charge them the tourist rate and give them a card to remind them that they had "done" this cathedral.

The walking is important because travelling is an essential part of pilgrimage, whether round the church, on a day trip to Canterbury Cathedral, or a major journey to Jerusalem, Rome or Santiago de Compostela. It is not that the longer a pilgrimage is the more "holy" it is; rather, my experience has been that, the longer the pilgrimage, the less chance you have to keep things neatly departmentalised. A good companion on the road is one who helps when the going gets tough, and not necessarily one who shares the same religious views. But, even on an Away Day to Canterbury Cathedral, the same principle applies. When the Bethnal Green churches made that journey last year, the participants were very aware that the context was spiritual, but we combined worship in the Cathedral with shopping, drinking and not a little fun on the bus. It was all part of the pilgrimage.

We have sought to create that sense of shared life at St John on Bethnal Green. Worship and prayer are at the centre of what we do, but we strive to ensure that this enables and encourages, rather than excluding. When we hold an art exhibition or a concert, we want an overlap — an intermingling — between the different uses of the building; we do not want either to pack away religion, as it were, in order to be a concert hall, nor do we want to tempt in an audience to hit them with religion. We want a space in which there is an opportunity for the church to be affected by the arts, and the arts to be affected by the church. From my particular perspective as the parish priest here, I would like to make the resources of the church (which includes both the building and the Christian traditions of prayer and spirituality) available to a much wider audience, not in order to shore up an outdated institution by finding a clever ploy to refill the pews, but rather to see what will happen next. I believe that those resources can be of real value, as shown by the continuing relevance of religious themes and symbols in contemporary art; but that we in the Church must allow for a dialogue in which we learn at least as much as we teach, and for new understandings and directions to emerge for the future of our Church.

This is the context in which Chris Gollon and I began to talk about a set of Stations of the Cross for St John's. Chris was exhibiting in a gallery just down the road in Bethnal Green, and I was drawn by the peculiar mixture of imagery that I saw in the paintings displayed in the window. Here were reflections of the local community's underbelly: wild party-goers, mad old men, dishevelled sex-workers and, amongst all of them, a constant vague hint of the presence of religion. These figures seemed to be people I knew well: people I bumped into in the streets and pubs; people who found their way to church to ask for money, food, a blessing; or who were themselves not sure why they were there at the Christmas Midnight Mass. Talking to Chris, it became clear he was drawn to exploring "outsiders" in his paintings and that religious symbolism and expression, drawn from painters like Goya, had enabled him to reveal these characters' inner depths. It reminded me of Jesus' description in Matthew 25 of the Last Judgement, where God declares that he is to be found amongst the poor, the despised and the outcast. What if we approached the Stations of the Cross from this perspective? So many versions remove the dirt, the humiliation, the pain that brought Jesus to the lowest level of humanity, just as so many churches seem to forget that this is where God is to be found now.

Chris' paintings suggested to me that he could explore the imagery of the Way of the Cross from this standpoint, without drifting into devotional explanation or security. However well we know the story, our pilgrimage through the Stations should include some of the challenge, the loss, the despair that Jesus' disciples felt as he made his way to his execution. Chris was very concerned that he was not a Christian; but the religious strands within his work showed an attention to, and an engagement with, issues of faith, religion and belief. In the same way that we had been trying to attract a wider group into sharing our church and its resources to see where the dialogue might lead us, so it seemed important to share this project with an artist who could come at the themes without the perspective of a settled faith. This did not feel like handing Jesus over to the Roman soldiers to get a good beating, but much more like inviting Simon of Cyrene to assist in carrying the cross! After all, Jesus was not afraid to associate with, and be looked after by, those who were not seen as good Jews — from uncouth shepherds and foreign travellers at his birth, through tax collectors and prostitutes, to the criminals crucified with him at his death. Those who approached Jesus and seem to have got the best responses from him were not the religious elite, but those with no particular religious standing who nevertheless recognised something special in him and presented themselves honestly. Chris has worked on this basis, exploring the themes of the Stations through his detailed knowledge of the artistic traditions, his fascination with the nature of humanity, and the discussions we have had about theology. This latter strand was not in order to tie Chris down to a particular theological direction, but to add another dimension to his palette, which he remained free to develop as he wished.

On this basis, Chris agreed to take on the commission. However, even before we started to consider how we might fund it, we needed to ensure that the church's congregation was behind it too. There would have been little point in starting a project that was designed to engage the wider community if we were not engaging the worshipping community as well. Our congregation is very diverse, and our Church Council (the elected body which has legal responsibility for managing the church's affairs) is representative of that diversity. Could we convince them that hanging fourteen of Chris' paintings in the church was a good idea? I was not entirely sure, but I was not prepared to ignore them, or push them into it. The project had to be owned by the people of the church, or else the whole idea of a shared pilgrimage of those praying the Stations mingling with those looking at the art would not be achieved.

I wanted the Council members to catch the vision that was exciting Chris and me, not to agree the content of each picture (which was fortunate, because Chris was not happy to work in that way); so we arranged for them to travel to Chris' studio to meet him and look at a range of his work. I remember being very anxious — the people of St John's are very kind to their clergy, but are certainly not afraid to disagree with them. But the day was full of serendipity. At the time, Chris had his studio on an island in the Thames, a little upstream from Hampton Court. It was a Saturday in the middle of summer, and we decided to make a day of it, travelling from Westminster Pier by boat. The journey took several hours but, on the river in glorious sunshine, we seemed to walk out of our daily lives into a slower, more beautiful world in which there was time to relax together, talk and enjoy each other's company. Another pilgrimage! And to an island — not just a studio in a row of buildings very much like our own neighbourhood. To be honest, it was not a very glamorous island in the middle of the Thames — but an island is an island and, combined with the boat trip, it worked its magic on us. After meeting Chris and David, his agent, the church members got to work exploring the canvasses around the rooms of the studio. My anxiety started to return. I realised that both Chris and David were terrified — that meeting the Church Council was, for them, rather like being interviewed on *Newsnight*. The lack of sketches of the Stations suddenly seemed like a grave mistake, particularly since Chris had no previous overtly religious art to display. I overheard comments from some expressing their dislike of style or images. It all seemed to be going very wrong, and the magic started to dissipate. In the discussion that followed, though, my fears proved groundless. The Council members took to Chris very quickly; his humility and the thoughtfulness with which he described his approach to our project encouraged them enormously and some — not, to be honest, those I had expected — had grasped the relationship between Chris' images of outsiders and Jesus' journey with his cross and expressed this with a spiritual depth and a passion I had not managed. As a result, even those who had not warmed to his style were very clear that the commission fitted with St John's and were very keen for it to go ahead. We had together reached the goal of our pilgrimage that day.

Not the final goal, however. The Church Council might have agreed to commission Chris, but we did not have the money to pay him. Finding sponsors has not been an easy task, and at times we have wondered if we would ever see fourteen completed Stations. That we have done so has been largely due to individuals, some from within the church, some from Chris' ever-widening circle of admirers and collectors, sharing in our vision and our pilgrimage. Each year, on Good Friday, we have come together to share in the journey of the Stations of the Cross, pausing at each, reading some prayers, singing a refrain and allowing the words, the prayers and the images to mingle together. At first, Chris' paintings were in the minority, providing just the start to our journey. As their number has grown, so has the number of those joining the group travelling around the church. Last year there were over two hundred and, as we have always hoped, a vast mixture — sharing the journey together, making room for those who wish to kneel, leaving space for those who want to spend longer at one painting, not judging and not excluding. Chris' paintings do not set out to be photographic; they require imagination, sensibility, emotion from us in response to them. With that engagement, as we mill round, trying to see over each other's shoulders, there is a sense of being part of the crowd that watched this man walk by. Now, as then, there is no unified response: the onlookers are free to make what they will of the things they see, but both those who engage with art and those who engage with Jesus Christ are opening themselves to be challenged and changed by what they see and experience. Another stage of a pilgrimage. And so we have changed the traditional geography of the paintings. It is usual that they end at the altar, the place of the celebration of the Eucharist — the place, therefore of resurrection. Our Stations end with the entombment of Jesus by the west door of the church. Some may return to celebrate the resurrection of Jesus at the altar, but all of us are led from the journey of the Stations of the Cross out into Bethnal Green, where we have to make sense of the things we have felt and seen. For Christians, this is where the truth of the resurrection is to be found too.

The Revd Alan Green is the Team Rector of St John on Bethnal Green. He came to the parish ten years ago after working in Liverpool and as Chaplain at Worcester College, Oxford. He is now the Area Dean of Tower Hamlets in the Diocese of London and chairs the Tower Hamlets Inter Faith Forum. He has twice made the pilgrimage to Santiago de Compostela in Spain by bicycle.

St John on Bethnal Green is a parish in London's inner East End, one of the most deprived areas of Britain. The population of the parish is highly diverse in terms of class, race and religious tradition. The church building, dedicated in 1828, is of major historical importance and Grade 1 Listed, having been designed by the eminent neo-classical architect Sir John Soane. It stands next to The Museum of Childhood in a very prominent position on a major crossroads in the centre of Bethnal Green.

Chris Gollon is an established name in British painting. Born in London in 1953, he has enjoyed many solo museum exhibitions in the UK, major museum acquisitions and public commissions. He has exhibited at Art Chicago and also with Yoko Ono, David Bowie and Gavin Turk in 'ROOT', a crossover exhibition of contemporary music and art created by Thurston Moore of Sonic Youth, at Chisenhale Gallery, London. His work is attracting increasing acclaim in the national press and specialist arts press. His film collaboration with JABOD, entitled 'Kaleidomorphism One', was premiered in London at the East End Film Festival (2008). A Fellow of the Institute of Advanced Study, University of Durham, Chris Gollon lives and works in Surrey, and is represented by IAP Fine Art, London.

Sara Maitland was born in 1950. Her first novel Daughter of Jerusalem *won the Somerset Maugham Award in 1979. Since then she has published five more novels and six collections of short stories. In March 2008 Maia Press published* Far North and Other Dark Tales *to celebrate the launch of the film "Far North", directed by Asif Kapadia and starring Michelle Yeoh and Sean Bean, which was based on that dark tale. She also writes non-fiction, particularly theology like* A Big Enough God *and* Angel and Me *(both from Continuum), and radio drama. Most recently* A Book of Silence *was published by Granta in 2008 to considerable critical acclaim.*